There he was.

He'd just come out of the barn, heading in her direction and pushing a triple stroller, the triplets lined up side by side.

She took him in, his tall, lean but muscular body, the thick dark short hair, clear blue eyes, strong jaw. She hadn't seen him close up like this in years, of course, and wow, was he good-looking.

"The *Cheyenne Daily Gazette* appreciates this special opportunity," she said with what had to be a strange smile plastered on her face. Could she be more awkward? *That* was her opening line? At least she didn't extend her hand. "I'm very sorry for your loss—and their loss," she said. "I never did get to say that to you."

"Well, we go way back," he said with a kind smile. "It's understood."

She appreciated that. "I guess this is a little... awkward."

"Trust me that the triplets have a way of commandeering any situation and taking the focus. There will be little time for awkward."

She smiled. "Good."

Her burning question would have to wait—*why* she was here at all. How he'd known she worked at the *Gazette*, why he'd cared to the point that he finally agreed to an interview—and on the condition that *she* write the story.

Dear Reader,

It's been six months since twenty-eight-year-old single rancher Nash Dawson became guardian of his orphaned triplet baby nephews. With a lot of love, help from family and on-the-go training in fatherhood, Nash finally feels like he knows what he's doing. But because his late brother was a famed rodeo star, all of Wyoming wants the story of how he and the triplets are doing. For good reasons, he's turned down every request for interviews and photos and video reels. Until now...

Junior reporter Wendy Watson is shocked when she hears that Nash Dawson has granted an exclusive interview to her. Former best friends, they haven't spoken in years. When she learns *why* he's entrusted her with the story, she's deeply touched. And suddenly, her entire life is about to change. But after time at the ranch with Nash and the triplets, everything Wendy thought she wanted is turned upside down...

I hope you enjoy Nash and Wendy's love story!

Warm wishes,

Melissa Senate

THE RANCHER'S FAMED TRIPLETS

MELISSA SENATE

SPECIAL EDITION

If you purchased this book without a cover you should be aware that this book is stolen property. It was reported as "unsold and destroyed" to the publisher, and neither the author nor the publisher has received any payment for this "stripped book."

MIX
Paper | Supporting responsible forestry
FSC® C021394

Harlequin® SPECIAL EDITION™

Recycling programs for this product may not exist in your area.

ISBN-13: 978-1-335-18024-7

The Rancher's Famed Triplets

Copyright © 2026 by Melissa Senate

All rights reserved. No part of this book may be used or reproduced in any manner whatsoever without written permission.

Without limiting the exclusive rights of any author, contributor or the publisher of this publication, any unauthorized use of this publication to train generative artificial intelligence (AI) technologies is expressly prohibited. Harlequin also exercises their rights under Article 4(3) of the Digital Single Market Directive 2019/790 and expressly reserves this publication from the text and data mining exception.

This is a work of fiction. Names, characters, places and incidents are either the product of the author's imagination or are used fictitiously. Any resemblance to actual persons, living or dead, businesses, companies, events or locales is entirely coincidental.

For questions and comments about the quality of this book, please contact us at CustomerService@Harlequin.com.

TM and ® are trademarks of Harlequin Enterprises ULC.

Harlequin Enterprises ULC
22 Adelaide St. West, 41st Floor
Toronto, Ontario M5H 4E3, Canada
www.Harlequin.com

HarperCollins Publishers
Macken House, 39/40 Mayor Street Upper,
Dublin 1, D01 C9W8, Ireland
www.HarperCollins.com

Printed in Lithuania

Melissa Senate has written many novels for Harlequin and other publishers, including her debut, *See Jane Date*, which was made into a TV movie. She also wrote seven books for Harlequin Special Edition under the pen name Meg Maxwell. Her novels have been published in over twenty-five countries. Melissa lives on the coast of Maine with her son; their rescue shepherd mix, Flash; and a lap cat named Cleo. For more information, please visit her website, melissasenate.com.

Books by Melissa Senate

Harlequin Special Edition

Montana Mavericks: Behind Closed Doors

The Maverick's Do-Over

Dawson Family Ranch

For the Twins' Sake
Wyoming Special Delivery
A Family for a Week
The Long-Awaited Christmas Wish
Wyoming Cinderella
Wyoming Matchmaker
His Baby No Matter What
Heir to the Ranch
Santa's Twin Surprise
The Cowboy's Mistaken Identity
Seven Birthday Wishes
Snowbound with a Baby
Triplets Under the Tree
The Rancher Hits the Road
The Cowboy's Christmas Redemption
The Rancher's Surprise Deal
The Baby's Christmas Ranch
The Rancher's Famed Triplets

Visit the Author Profile page
at Harlequin.com for more titles.

For my son, Max, with all my love.

Chapter One

All three triplets were finally napping. Nash Dawson stood by his nephew Dallas's crib, almost unable to believe the peaceful baby with the serene expression and quirking lower lip had been screaming his head off two minutes ago. Dallas had woken up his brothers twice during his battle to stay awake, but those two always fell back to sleep easily. Dallas didn't like to miss a thing, even if that was just his Uncle Nash singing him an off-key lullaby with the words wrong.

Nash looked down at the babies in their pj's, Dallas in orange, Ryder in blue, Callum in green. Nash could easily tell them apart but they were always color-coded in orange, blue and green as a just-in-case; the triplets were fraternal but looked so much alike that Nash's dad often mixed up who was who. "Love you guys," he whispered, unable to move away or tear his gaze from their beautiful, serene faces, their little chests rising and falling. His precious nephews.

Next week would mark six months that he'd become their legal guardian.

Six months since Nash's brother and sister-in-law

and her parents were killed in a private plane crash on their way home from a rodeo across Wyoming.

How tiny the triplets had been then, just one month old, Nash scared to death at the breadth of the responsibility. And Nash Dawson had always been a responsible person—even as a kid dutifully doing his barn chores before school. *I*'s dotted, *t*'s crossed, ducks in a row—all of it. But taking on the care of his three orphaned nephews—nothing he'd ever been through had prepared him for what would be involved. Just the basics of getting a baby—times three—through a day on earth.

Until Dallas, Ryder and Callum had come to live with him at the ranch, Nash, at twenty-eight years old, had never:

1. Changed a diaper.
2. Given a baby a bottle.
3. Been woken by a screaming infant at 3:00 a.m.
4. Sung a lullaby—or googled the lyrics to a lullaby.
5. Wrangled little arms legs and heads into onesies and footsie pajamas.
6. Bathed a baby.
7. Burped a baby.
8. Been thrown up on.
9. Canceled plans because of a baby.
10. Ended a relationship because of *three* babies.

There was more, from taking a baby's temperature to squeezing medication into sore ears. Rubbing ointment on gums about to erupt with a first tooth. Rushing a baby or two or three to their pediatrician or the urgent care because of a high fever or a cough that sounded like a tractor.

Learning what the triplets needed only for it to change the following month. Remembering what calming tricks worked on what baby. Wrangling schedules that didn't always line up. Case in point: Dallas taking twenty minutes longer to fall asleep than his brothers.

Amazingly, Nash had figured it out as he went, something that had seemed so beyond him those first days and weeks. And now, six months after becoming their guardian, he would even say he actually knew what he was doing. He was no pro, but he did get through the day. And at the long end of it, the triplets always magically looked exactly as they did now: happy, healthy, peaceful. And asleep.

What he would *never* get used to was the depth of his love for these boys. Had he been pacing with frustration just five minutes ago, rubbing screaming Dallas's back, sending up prayers to the universe that the baby would fall asleep like his brothers?

All that, like all the hard parts of taking care of these little guys, was a distant memory. What burned brightly was the *love*.

And the promise he'd made them the day their lives had all changed. A promise he'd also made to the memory of his late brother, sister-in-law and her parents. To be everything the triplets needed and deserved, which was the world. Nash would not let them down.

Not letting them down required so much constant learning, so much effort, so much of him that sometimes Nash didn't think he *would* get through the day.

And that was even with help, thanks to his salt-of-the-earth parents and grandmother, his excellent cowboy and ranch hand who always went the extra mile, and kind neighbors who he could call in a pinch.

Every minute of every day Nash was so busy between the ranch and the triplets that the fear he still had of screwing up at baby care couldn't get inside his head until he was in bed at night, baby monitor on his bedside table. But what always seemed to be with him, what he couldn't shake, what he'd told *no one*, not even his grandmother who he was very close with, was his final conversation with his brother.

The day before his death. A phone call that Nash wished with everything in him had gone differently.

Nash turned away from the three cribs and closed his eyes, his brother's face coming to mind. The trademark Dawson dark hair, blue eyes, ever-present Stetson. Ethan had had a dimple unlike Nash, and an easy smile that showed it off. That was how he pictured his brother right now, brim down low, the warm smile.

His heart clenched and he tried to let out the breath lodged in his throat but it always got stuck.

He'd had words with his brother, words he wished every damned day he could take back—and then the next day, Ethan Dawson was gone.

Nash let his head drop back and tried, as always, when he got assailed by this memory, to fill his mind with other things, and there was always a lot right there to swoop in. Such as the triplets' seven-month well-baby checkup and remembering to remind his mother about accompanying him, not that Polly Dawson forgot anything. Thank God for his mom. He didn't know what he'd do without his family.

The phone rang just then, solving the problem of clearing his head. He hurried out to his bedroom since Dallas woke at anything, whereas the other two could generally sleep through a herd of racing bulls. If Dallas woke, getting him back to sleep would take another twenty minutes, and Nash needed to use this time to go over the ranch's invoices and inventory needs.

He had a landline upstairs in his bedroom and downstairs in the kitchen, just part of the attempt to baby-ize his life in case of this or that. He grabbed the phone from his bedside table, relieved that Dallas hadn't made a peep.

The second Nash said hello and then heard, "Good afternoon, Mr. Dawson, this is Allen McCrane with…" he shook his head and inwardly groaned. Dammit.

Why the hell had Nash thought it was safe to answer the landline? The past few weeks, the calls from the media had started up again. Nothing like the way the phone had constantly rung in those early days and weeks after the crash. Nash's brother had been a popular rodeo champion and every regional newspaper, magazine, TV show, radio station and podcast had requested interviews with Nash, wanting to capitalize on the story of the tragic loss of Wyoming's home-state hero, the sad orphaned triplets and the single rancher who'd taken them in.

He'd also been offered promotional deals to hawk everything from diapers to beer with the triplets photographed in cowboy hats and onesies with lassos.

Nash had said a firm no to every request—his nephews weren't a moneymaking sideshow. His brother had had fans all over the west and Nash knew that people had loved Ethan. And yeah, maybe it was a human-interest story most people did care about. But there was no way he'd let his family tragedy sell newspapers or build viewership. "In your brother's memory…" the media had all unsuccessfully pleaded with faux reverence.

Unintentionally always reminding Nash of his last conversation with his brother. One he couldn't change—and somehow had to live with for the rest of his life.

For a few months now, the requests for interviews had dwindled to the point that Nash had stopped walking around expecting the phone to blow up and watching for strangers, the media and his brother's well-meaning fans coming to the ranch "in support." Neighbors, even those he hadn't known personally, also often had dropped by with condolences, stuffed animals and so much food that Nash had had to buy a separate freezer. But with the six-month mark since his brother died approaching, the requests had started up again for interviews, photos, video footage. Nash had turned down everyone all over again, and reminded himself to not answer the landline since his cell had always been safe from the hordes.

And now someone named Allen McCrane was yakking in his ear. "Executive Editor of the *Cheyenne Daily Gazette*," the man continued. He went on about the newspaper's circulation and reach—as if Nash gave a damn—the prizes and awards, both local and national, and that the *Gazette* had been named the region's most trusted news source in local polls five years running. "I know that next week will mark six months since the tragic loss of Wyoming's favorite rodeo champ, Ethan Dawson, and his wife and her parents. Our hearts are all very heavy. Our readers would be so comforted to hear how the triplets are doing, how their uncle is doing as their legal guardian. Oh, what just a photo of those little champs would do for the morale of the good folks of Cheyenne and all of Wyoming. It would be a front-page story, Mr. Dawson."

The editor took a breath, pausing, likely gearing up to hear Nash say that he would not grant an interview or photos, *sorry*, *bye*.

But along with annoyance and flat-out disdain, something else had suddenly crashed into Nash's thoughts. *Someone*.

Wendy Watson.

He hadn't spoken to Wendy since they were thirteen and had gone from best friends to...not acknowledging each other in the hallways at school or at 4-H club or at the ice-cream or pizza place or coffee shop in Bear Ridge. He'd barely seen her since she left town at eighteen for college. He'd occasionally catch a glimpse of her long red hair in town and for a split second his heart would swell—there was his childhood best friend—but then he'd remember they'd long been strangers. She hated him and he didn't blame her.

Just a few days ago, Nash had run into Wendy Watson's mother in the grocery store while his parents were babysitting the triplets. Nash had been in the bread aisle when he heard someone call his name. Andrea Watson. Tall and redhaired like Wendy, her mom grabbed both his hands and asked after him and the triplets, then started launching into complaint after complaint about her daughter.

How "selfish and self-absorbed" Wendy had broken her parents' hearts by running off to supposedly greener pastures to chase her dream of being an investigative journalist instead of working at the family farm. And how seven years later, she was "just an assistant reporter covering basic stories she could do right here in Bear Ridge." Mrs. Watson had gone on to add that at least Wendy had gotten hired a few months ago at the respected *Cheyenne Daily Gazette*. "But Watson Dairy has needed her all these years," she'd said, shaking her head. "At least her sister loves the farm. I don't know what I'd do without Tess."

Nash had waited for the woman to finally take a breath, then said, "I used to feel that way about my brother, Mrs. Watson. Ethan left the family ranch, left us all high and dry to chase his dream of being a champion bronc rider. But when he died, I realized I was glad he'd gone after his dream."

Mrs. Watson had lifted her chin, her expression a strange mix of compassion and *you're wrong*. "Yeah, but Ethan *achieved* his dream. Big difference."

Actually, no, it wasn't a big difference. Or a difference that mattered. The *pursuit* was important. The *trying*. Life was short. *Go for what will make you truly happy.* He understood that now.

"It's too bad you and Wendy never fixed whatever went wrong between you two," Mrs. Watson had plowed on as though he and Wendy hadn't stopped speaking fifteen years ago. "You would have made such a nice couple. Wendy is *still* single. Not a grandchild on the horizon, humph." Someone at the end of the aisle caught her eye and she waved at the person, then said, "So nice to see you, Nash." Then with a hand to her heart, she added, "You take good care of those little boys." And then she was thankfully off.

He'd stood there in the bread aisle, unsettled, his heart going out to Wendy Watson despite the fact that they *hadn't* said a word to each other since they were thirteen. *She's trying*, he'd wished he'd had a chance to say to her mother.

And good for you, Wendy, he thought now. *Out there, chasing your dreams. That takes courage—to believe in yourself.*

Back when they were still friends, Wendy used to often talk about her problems with her mother. How critical she was, how judgmental, how she made Wendy feel ashamed of herself for just being who she was. He and Wendy would talk about it and he'd do what he could to make her feel better or forget her mom altogether while they were swimming in the creek or exploring a mountain cave or sharing an order of large fries at the Bear Ridge Diner.

But then a stupid incident—something he also wished he could take back—destroyed that friendship.

If Wendy Watson had any idea that her mother had told him all about her life now, right in the middle of the grocery store, she'd be mortified. So many memories of the two of them when they were five, seven, ten, twelve…right on up to that year of boy-girl parties at thirteen that had changed everything hit him dead in the chest. She'd been his best friend. And he'd ruined it. Hurt her.

Now, with unexpected thanks to his mother being who she was, he realized he could do something for Wendy. Something helpful.

Everyone in Wyoming wanted the interview with the single guardian uncle of the poor orphaned triplet sons of rodeo champ Ethan Dawson. Maybe giving Wendy the story and byline would right some old wrongs on many levels.

His stomach twisted some, but Nash said, "I'll grant the *Gazette* an in-depth interview and allow photos on *one* condition. That you send reporter Wendy Watson to do the story. I like her work."

Or he had in middle school, when she'd been the star reporter of the school newspaper and wrote about rubbery chicken nuggets in the cafeteria needing an adjustment and how the school day should start a half hour later so that young minds could refuel.

"Mr. Dawson, I'm absolutely honored," the editor said. "But Wendy Watson is so *junior*. Surely you want a seasoned—"

"I gave you my one condition," Nash interrupted. "Wendy can arrive at the ranch for the interview at her convenience."

The editor gushed his thanks and they said their goodbyes.

He went back into the nursery to check on the triplets. They were all still asleep, even Dallas. "For Wendy," he whispered, knowing they'd understand why he'd said yes to an article and a few photos after six months of a hard no.

He'd long been telling the triplets everything except of course about that last conversation with their father. Or anything about his relationship with Ethan. Nash would never say anything remotely negative to the triplets about their dad, no matter how old they were—a month or six months or thirty years old. His and Ethan's issues had been their own. *Nash's* issues, he'd come to realize.

But when it came to everything else going on in his life, he rambled to the triplets because they *were* just babies. Nothing was too banal or too important, from his hopes for them to his fears, to his work day or the lunch he was preparing, to his own dreams. And they listened politely, sometimes lately bursting out with a laugh or a babbled sound or two. *Ba-la.*

The day he'd gotten back from the grocery store, excited about introducing them to more solid foods this week, he'd told them all about the conversation with Wendy Watson's mother. And filled them in on every detail of his and Wendy's friendship—and how they'd gone from the closest of friends to *nothing* with one stupid move. He'd screwed up—and then he'd screwed that up too by not handling the aftermath well. An understatement.

They'd stared at him with big blue eyes, curious. And then Callum had started waving his chew toy around. Ryder had let out a *ba!* And Dallas had started crying.

God, he loved these babies. And he knew they'd understand years from now, when they looked through old documents in the attic and saw a *Gazette* article about them, about the loss of their parents and maternal grandparents, about what life was like living with their Uncle Nash back when they were six months old.

"For Wendy," he whispered again, hoping with everything in him that he wouldn't regret this—on a few different levels.

Wendy Watson sat at her desk in the bullpen of the *Cheyenne Daily Gazette*, working on an article about a twenty-year-old cat that had been rescued from a tree by a ten-year-old neighbor. Among her many duties, Wendy handled the Good Samaritan feature for the People in the News page and wrote up two short articles a day from nominations emailed in.

She took a sip of her take-out coffee and a bite of her cranberry muffin and glanced around the busy newsroom, her fellow reporters typing away or on the phone with sources. As always, her heart gave a happy leap. She was *here*. Writing a story about a cat stuck in a tree, but she was writing it at the *Gazette*. A major step on the ladder to her dream.

Since graduating with a journalism degree from Wyoming State seven years ago, she'd paid her dues at any newspaper that would give her a chance, her collection of clips getting her to papers with higher circulations than the last, but never a major paper. Until now. Her breaking story on a school board scandal at the newspaper she worked at prior, which had taken investigative work, multiple sources, long nights of research and painstaking fact-checking on her part, had finally caught the attention of the *Gazette*'s news editor. Three months ago, when she'd been hired, she thought she was on her way. But she'd either been assigned to do research for more senior reporters or to write the basic stories no one else wanted to cover. Like the Good Samaritan feature. She loved those stories from a reader perspective—just not as the reporter.

She took another gulp of coffee, then read over the intro paragraph of the Good Samaritan feature, which was solid in her opinion. Her boss liked that she put personal touches into human interest pieces like this one, such as making a cute quip about the cat's name, Ebony, despite her snow-white fur, and how her owner had realized she'd slipped out when he clinked a spoon on her bowl of Fancy Feast and Ebony hadn't come running. The ten-year-old girl next door had offered to help, looked up and saw Ebony on a branch of the tree in the front yard. She'd climbed up, scooped up the cat and came back down her elderly neighbor's hero. The grateful cat owner had found his way to the paper's online Good Samaritan submission form, and Wendy had been charmed by the story. She had to get her picks approved before writing them, but her boss seemed to like all her choices.

Put your heart and soul into every article you write as a reporter, no matter what the subject or if it's on page one or buried on page twenty-seven—that was her dad's advice when Wendy left home for her first job as a reporter.

Assistant reporter, her mother had corrected.

Wendy sighed at the memory. Seven years later, her mother hadn't changed a bit, making snide comments and outright complaining that Wendy was wasting her time on this "career choice" when the family farm could use her help.

Thank God for her father, whose support meant the world to Wendy. He knew that becoming a hard-hitting investigative journalist, ending up in a big city like New York or Chicago or Los Angeles, had been her dream since she was in elementary school and contributed articles to the school paper. By middle school, Wendy knew she'd major in journalism in college and aspire to become an investigative reporter. And after college, she'd taken her father's advice and put everything she had into every story she was assigned. The grunt work, the hard work, would pay off. Wendy had always believed that. It had gotten her to the *Gazette* and with time, her work and work *ethic* would get her bigger stories. She just had to be patient.

Her phone pinged with a text—from Janna Lopez. Her boss.

Wendy, can you pop by right now?

Right now? That was unusual. She typed back Be right there! and then sucked in a breath. What could this possibly be about? Was she getting fired? A slightly more senior reporter who worked the police beat had been let go yesterday for a mistake in a story along with the fact-checker who'd missed the error.

Wendy swallowed. She gulped down the rest of her coffee, then got up and hurried to her boss's office. Could she have messed up somewhere? She wracked her brain, but nothing came to mind.

She paused at her boss's office. Janna looked up and waved her in, gesturing for her to sit in the guest chair facing her desk. In her fifties with a trademark low bun and round silver eyeglasses, Janna was a godsend as a boss—a warm mentor, yet also no nonsense, and truly seeming to care about the three journalists who reported to her.

"I have a big assignment for you, Wendy," Janna said, her dark eyes assessing. "We're talking front page."

Wendy felt her eyes widen. Front page? *Her?*

"The assignment's come down from the big boss," Janna added. "*Everyone* would want this story, even me. But it's yours. Run with it like I know you will."

Wendy was stunned silent for a moment. Why on earth would Allen McCrane, executive editor of the *Cheyenne Daily Gazette*, skip over everyone, including the news editor herself, for a *front page* story?

"You've only been with the *Gazette* a few months," Janna said, "but you know from the last staff meeting that we've been trying to score an interview with rodeo champ Ethan Dawson's brother—the single rancher who took in his three orphaned baby nephews. For the past *six months*. Heck, I've called him three times myself over that time. Allen's called him *four* times. Nash Dawson turned down *all* requests."

Wendy's heart pinched at the thought of Nash. He'd lost his brother, his sister-in-law and his in-laws. And with that heartrending tragedy, he'd become the legal guardian of one-month-old orphaned triplets.

She hadn't spoken to Nash since they were thirteen but no one had to tell her that he'd not only stepped up but had given the triplets his all. He might have broken her heart in more ways than one but he hadn't become an instant jerk that day long ago. She'd been so devastated by the end of their friendship because she'd known *exactly* what she'd lost in him.

Janna took a sip of her green smoothie. "Well, Allen tried for a fifth time today since the six-month mark is coming up next week, and it seems Nash Dawson has had a change of heart about granting the *Gazette* an interview. On the condition that *you're* the reporter on the story."

Wendy gasped and leaned forward. "*Me?*"

"That was exactly Allen's reaction. What's your connection to Nash Dawson?"

We used to be best friends. But there hasn't been a connection in fifteen years. "I grew up in Bear Ridge," she explained. "I used to be friends with Nash and his brother way back when."

"Ah," her boss said. "That answers that. A hometown connection can be powerful. Well, Nash Dawson says you can arrive for the story at your convenience. We'd like to get you out there tomorrow. Spend a few days in town, get an in-depth interview and some great photos, plus a few short videos. Do that, Wendy, and Allen has basically told me it'll earn you a promotion to full reporter."

Wendy gasped again.

Janna nodded and leaned forward herself. "This story will be picked up by every paper in the state—and the west. Ethan Dawson was our state superstar. When word came that he'd died with his wife and in-laws, that those one-month-old triplet boys were orphaned—everyone's heart went out to them and Nash Dawson. A single rancher who took them in, his life completely changed in an instant."

Single… Every time Wendy had gone home to visit her family over the years, she'd kept her ears perked for news about Nash Dawson's marital status. Not that she'd harbored any thoughts about the two of them ever becoming a couple. She was just aware, as she'd been since the last time they'd spoken, that she'd always care about him. Always wonder. And if she'd heard he *had* gotten married? That he'd fallen in love, that someone had stolen his heart? It would probably sting. The first boy she'd ever loved. She'd never had a chance with him and she never would.

But why he'd done her this big favor was beyond her. Nash had turned down every media outlet during the past six months but now said yes if *she'd* do the reporting? And how on earth had Nash Dawson even known where she worked? Cheyenne was hours away from Bear Ridge.

"Do a great job with this assignment and it's your ticket," Janna added. "And congratulations. This is how life works. You just never know when something amazing will fall into your lap. What is that saying—luck is when preparation meets opportunity? Like I said, Wendy—run with it."

Wendy was dimly aware of nodding and her boss telling her to spend the next couple of hours doing her research on the Dawsons and to be at the ranch first thing in the morning. Because "don't ranchers wake up with the roosters? Get to Nash Dawson while he's fresh and well rested and unlikely to change his mind."

Get to Nash Dawson. Words Wendy never thought would have anything to do with her again.

Chapter Two

At the turn to the Dawson Brothers Cattle Ranch, named by Nash's grandparents for their then two young sons, and so fitting for the next *two* generations of sons, Nash and Ethan, and then the triplets, Wendy sucked in a breath and actually pulled over to give herself a minute.

She was going to see Nash Dawson, talk to him for the first time in fifteen years. And not just small talk because of running into him in line at the coffee shop or on the sidewalk in town. She'd be interviewing him, asking personal questions, spending an intense few days with him and the triplets. That would be *some* reunion.

It's perfect, her sister, Tess, had said last night when Wendy had arrived at Watson Dairy. *You'll get to bury the hatchet with Nash and earn a promotion at the same time!*

True. Both were welcome. But Wendy had such butterflies about seeing Nash. She'd thought of him often over the years, particularly six months ago when she'd heard the terrible news about his brother. She'd ached for him that day. And now, sitting in her car, glancing at herself in the rearview mirror to check that her hair hadn't blown askew or that a piece of the bagel she'd had for breakfast wasn't stuck in her teeth, she knew she was nervous in an excited way.

Fifteen years hadn't quelled those old feelings, she supposed. Maybe because he'd been her best friend for years, her confidant, and then she'd clammed up with people after that. Nash Dawson held both a special place deep inside and a hurtful place. Perhaps that kind of first love stuff, even unrealized first love, never went away.

Last night at the farm had been wonderful. Wendy had arrived just past 10:00 p.m, and it had been only her and sister at the two-bedroom cabin that Tess lived in on Watson Dairy, just down the path from the main house where they'd grown up. Tess had turned the cabin into a cozy home for herself, and given the long drive, her nerves and the late hour, Wendy had opted to stay with her sister, who'd also always supported her, and not her parents, though that would probably give her mother something to complain about when she found out today. She had no idea how her mom would react to the news that she'd gotten a big assignment, particularly one that had brought her home to Bear Ridge. Andrea Watson would find something negative or snide to say and it would have Wendy popping a TUMS, as it always did.

She'd visit with her parents sometime today. At least she could count on her dad to be supportive and proud of her.

Now it was just before 9:00 a.m, which seemed a

reasonable hour to show up for a professional visit. Her boss had said before she left her office that Allen would let Nash know to expect Wendy this morning.

"Okay, let's go," she told herself, putting her SUV back into Drive. She turned onto the dirt road for the Dawson Brothers Cattle Ranch, her heart starting to pound. This was a double big deal and as long as her nerves didn't show when she got out of her vehicle, she'd be fine.

As she drove up the road, the white farmhouse came into view with its pretty red door and black shutters, a red barn a quarter mile away where the pastures and open fields were, cattle dotting the landscape.

And as she got closer, she gasped, her hand flying to her chest.

There he was.

He'd just come out of the barn, heading in her direction, and pushing a triple stroller, the triplets lined up side by side. He stopped as if he also needed to brace himself, then kept walking. When she could see him more clearly, she realized he was talking. She supposed to the triplets.

She sucked in another breath and got out of the car into the beautiful May weather, a lovely morning at sixty-two degrees. He held up a hand in greeting as he neared her, and she did the same.

They both seemed to freeze for a second. Because of the awkwardness, she figured. The strange situation. She took him in, his tall lean but muscular body, the thick dark short hair, clear blue eyes, strong jaw. He wore a dark brown Stetson, a long-sleeved flannel Western shirt, jeans and work boots. She hadn't seen him close up like this in years of course and, wow, was he good-looking. She could still see that boy she'd adored in his face, her bestie, but the butterflies flapping around were for the man he was now, the stranger.

"The *Cheyenne Daily Gazette* appreciates this special opportunity," she said with what had to be a strange smile plastered on her face. Could she be more awkward? *That* was her opening line? At least she hadn't extended her hand.

She looked down at the three adorable babies in the stroller. They were definitely Dawsons—with their thick brown hair and blue eyes. She could see they weren't identical triplets but they sure did look alike. She kneeled in front. "Well, hello there," she said to them. "I'm Wendy Watson."

Nash moved to the left. "And this is Dallas." He moved back to the center. "This is Ryder." Now to the right. "And this here is Callum." *Dallas in orange, Ryder in blue, Callum in green.* She committed that to memory. By tomorrow she was sure she'd be able to connect their faces with their names no matter what colors they were in.

"Ba!" Callum said.

Ryder let out an enormous giggle that had Wendy laughing too.

She eyed Dallas, who was staring at her with his big blue eyes. Not a peep. Reserving judgment, perhaps.

"I'm so happy to meet you three," she said with a smile. For a moment she was struck by all they'd been through when they were just a month old. The loss of their parents and maternal grandparents, moving in with their uncle, the entire trajectory of their lives changed in a heartbeat. She stood and faced Nash. "I'm very sorry for your loss—and their loss," she said. "I never did get to say that to you."

"Well, we go way back," he said with a kind smile. "It's understood."

She appreciated that. "I guess this is a little... awkward. When I woke up yesterday morning and got ready for work, I certainly didn't expect that the next day, I'd be *here*."

"Same," he said. "But as for the awkward, trust me that the triplets have a way of commandeering any situation and taking the focus. There will be little time for awkward."

She smiled. "Good."

And just then, as if on cue, the middle triplet, Ryder, started rubbing his eyes. Then Dallas let out something of a cry. Only Callum seemed content at the moment. The word *moment* being key since suddenly Callum started fussing, twisting his little body a bit.

Her burning question would have to wait—*why* she was here at all. How he'd known she worked at the *Gazette*, why he'd cared to the point that he finally agreed to an interview—and on the condition that *she* write the story.

"Wow," she said, eyeing the babies. "They must be a lot."

He gave a laugh. "A lot of everything."

"Can you expand on that?" she asked, pulling out her phone. "Do you mind if I record our conversation?"

He frowned. "Actually, yes, I do mind. And it's time to get these rug rats into the bathtub since they were happily crawling in their little fenced pasture a little while ago. Then nap time. We could get the interview taken care of then. An hour would likely suffice, don't you think?"

Now *she* frowned. She'd already screwed up. The man clearly wasn't comfortable about interviews and photos and videos. And here she was, practically shoving a microphone in his face within a minute of arriving. She sucked in a quick breath, trying to figure out the right thing to say. *Be yourself, Wendy.*

"Sorry," she said. "I'm so truly interested in how you've managed, Nash, so I got a little ahead of myself. But yes, the questions can wait."

And an *hour*? Was that all he'd give her? Her boss seemed to expect her to stick around for a few days, spending lots of time with Nash and the triplets. Not a quick sit-down interview during nap time. More like going about his life with them, observing, asking natural questions, taking it all in so she could let it all pour out on paper.

He didn't frown again, but his eyes narrowed. "Interested as a reporter." He shook his head. "Forget I said that. It's why you're here."

She tilted her head, trying to understand him, but coming up short. Did he *want* her to be interested as someone he used to know? His former best friend?

This was complicated for her and had to be for him as well.

So first things first. Comfort level.

"About the interview," she said. "How about this—we're *off* the record until I ask if we can be on. That way you don't have to wonder or worry about what you say."

He extended a hand. "I appreciate that." She glanced at his hand—no ring—and then shook. His warm strong fingers enveloped hers, the touch sending the slightest shock waves to her nerve endings.

Once I was closer to you than to my own sister, she thought suddenly. *Of course this...reunion has me completely off-kilter.*

"All right, guys," he directed toward the babies. "Time for your baths. I'd normally call one of my parents or my grandmother to see if they're in the mood to help with bath time, but since you're here, it's certainly a perfect way to see how I *do* manage. If I manage," he added with a smile.

She smiled back. "I'd love to help. Although it would be a first. I've never bathed a baby before. They're not slippery, are they?"

He raised an eyebrow. "Well, yes." He chuckled. "Now you sound like me that first week I became their guardian. I was so afraid I'd break them. Drop one on his head. Or that I'd turn *my* head to see why one was crying, and the other would be in some mortal danger because I looked away for a split second." He mock-shivered. "I would not want to go back to those days."

"Well, it was coupled with intense grief too," she said. How incredibly painful and difficult that time must have been.

He looked at her, thoughtfully, and nodded. "Exactly that."

Just as she was about to wonder how he'd get that giant stroller up the three wide porch steps, she realized there was a ramp on the side, which he pushed the stroller up. She went up the stairs.

"If you don't mind getting the door," he said. "Which I expanded, by the way. This used to be a normal door. Now this thing can easily fit through. I used to have a choo-choo train style stroller but at three months, when they were so curious and wide-eyed about their surroundings, I switched to this behemoth so that two of them wouldn't always be staring at the back of the seat in front of them."

She wondered if the stroller was heavy to push. She was sure she'd find out during her time with the Dawsons. She headed to the beautiful wide wood door and opened it, stepping inside and pulling the door aside so that Nash could push through the stroller. "I can only imagine how many things had to change here."

"Namely me," he said.

She wanted to rush at him with her questions. Not in reporter mode. In Wendy mode. Old friend mode. Starting-over mode.

He set the stroller to the side near a bench with cubbies and hooks for jackets, then plucked two babies from the stroller.

"Why don't you take Callum," he said. "And I'll get the other two. It's more natural than you might think to pick up a baby."

She bent down and smiled at the little guy. "Hi, there. I'm going to take you to your bath, if that's okay."

Nash laughed, and she smiled.

"I guess I sound a little formal," she said, unbuckling the harness, which was easy enough, and sticking her hands under the little one's arms and then cuddling him to her chest. "Aww, he's so light. Yet sturdy at the same time."

"I remember being in total wonder about that," he said. "The nursery and their bathroom are up there." He headed toward the stairs, a baby in each arm.

She walked slowly, holding Callum as tightly as she could without squishing him. She followed Nash up the stairs, remembering well running up and down it, the family photos lining the wall. Back then of course there'd been the parents and grandparents and two children, Nash and Ethan. But now the photos showed the Dawson brothers as older teens, Nash on college graduation day with his degree in agricultural management, Ethan on his bronc, Ethan's wedding photos, his wife and the triplets.

The gallery was a tribute to the family but she knew it must be hard for Nash to walk past these photos every day. Back when they were kids and teenagers, she remembered that Nash and his brother were often at odds. According to Nash, Ethan, older by two years, always made excuses for not doing his chores around the ranch, talking nonstop about his bronc-riding classes and camps and how one day he'd be a champ. Nash, definitely the more grounded and responsibly minded of the two, used to grouse about picking up his older brother's slack. She figured they'd gotten closer as they'd aged. After all, Nash was the one named guardian of the triplets.

Another of her long list of questions. How that had come about. A single twenty-eight-year-old taking on three infants? She didn't know much about the triplets' mother's relatives, other than that her parents had been tragically lost in the plane crash as well. In due time, once she and Nash found their rhythm as interviewer and subject, she was sure she'd get all her questions answered. But right now, it was bath time.

She followed Nash past more family photos lining the upstairs hallway walls into the large bathroom, Callum staring at her with huge blue eyes. He was so unbelievably cute, particularly up close like this. His cheeks were enormous. And the way he stared at her, latching onto her face with such interest. Nash set Ryder and Dallas into a playpen under the arched window and she put their brother beside them.

"One of the first things I learned," he said. "A playpen in every room is a must. Including the kitchen. The need to set one or two or all three down in a safe place comes up *constantly*."

As she watched him turn on the water and test it with his fingers, then take the three stacked baby tubs from a shelving unit and set them side by side in the big tub, filling each with water and a squirt of wonderfully smelling baby wash, she could see what he meant. He'd need two hands and babies who were safe. "I only ever bathe one a time to avoid getting distracted, but we can do two together with two sets of eyes and hands."

She smiled and watched him pluck Ryder from the

playpen. Nash deftly got him undressed, put the diaper in some kind of little trash can–like contraption, and then set the baby in the first tub. Ryder immediately grinned and batted at the water.

"Luckily, they all love bath time," he said.

She took Dallas out since she'd already bonded a little with Callum, and did exactly what Nash had. Dallas let out an impossibly loud laugh from such a little body as he batted the water, bubbles floating up.

Wendy laughed with him, that sound infectious. She appreciated the mini tubs, which helped keep the babies more secure than sitting them down in the big tub. She followed Nash's moves, rubbing a little baby shampoo in her hands and soaping up Dallas, including his hair. He smelled delicious. Then, keeping a hand firmly on the baby, she took a brightly colored little pail from the rim of the tub and filled it with fresh water from the lightly running tap. As Nash had, she used her hand as a shield above his eyes and gently poured the water over his head, rinsing off the soap. He seemed to love that too. Ryder however, clearly did not want water poured over his head at that moment because he started screaming bloody murder.

"Fussbudget," Nash said with a smile, scooping him out. On hooks right by the tub were three baby towels with hoods that had adorable animal ears—a panda, tiger and cat. He wrapped Ryder in the panda towel, the baby so adorable with the little bear ears sticking up. Ryder piped down pretty quickly. Nash took him over to the changing table against the wall and put on a fresh diaper, then grabbed pj's from a shelf and slipped the baby into those. "Voila. Bathed and changed." He set clean Ryder in the playpen, putting a chewy rattle in front of him, then scooped up Callum. "Your turn, my man."

Wendy smiled and grabbed the cat towel, then realized she needed to pick up Dallas, then wrap him. The tiniest things were big things in babyland. She got Dallas over to the changing table and laid him down as if she had any idea how to diaper a baby. Two of her girlfriends had babies, but she'd only held them a couple of times and briefly.

Wendy was a smart woman and would figure it out. Keeping a hand on Dallas, she reached below onto the shelf for a diaper from the stack. One side of the diaper was higher so she positioned that in the back. Success! She secured the tabs, not too tightly. Not a peep from the kiddo, so she figured she had it on all right.

"Great job," he said. "You've clearly done this before."

"Beginner's luck. I've never been anywhere near a diaper."

He laughed, soaping up Callum's hair. "You're a natural then. I sure wasn't." He shook his head thoughtfully, and she could tell he was thinking back.

"If I may ask *on* the record," she said. "How long would you say it took you to feel like you knew what you were doing? I ask both as a reporter and as your old friend."

"My parents and grandmother kept assuring me I was doing much better than I thought I was. The littlest thing would rattle me because I wanted to do right by the triplets."

"Aww, I'm sure," she said, watching as he wrapped Callum in the bear towel and cuddled him for a moment, leaning her head against the hood's ears.

"I learned fast because I had to, but it took a while before I felt really comfortable, like I really knew what I was doing. In between night wakings, I'd watch YouTube videos on baby care tutorials."

Wendy's heart pinged for him. "Your parents and grandmother must have been a huge help. They're such kind, warm people. What a support system." His mother had always been so kind to her, so interested in her opinions and asking her what she'd learned in school that day or what stories she was working on for the school newspaper. Wendy had always felt like her own mom didn't like her. Loved her, sure. But being a constant source of disappointment for as long as Wendy could remember used to make her wish Andrea Watson had been more like Polly Dawson.

"Definitely," he said as he headed over to the changing table. "They've had to slow down though. My mom had a heart attack two years ago that scared the stuffing out of us. And my dad got thrown from a horse last year and walks with a cane. They needed to move into the foreman's cabin that I used to live in because it's all one level. It's a great space for them though—three bedrooms, very cozy. *And* they get a break from the twenty-four-seven of baby triplets while being right down the path."

"Oh, wow," she said. "Sounds like they help with

the triplets as much as they can, but the onus really falls on you—and you're likely worrying about *them* too."

He nodded. As he was about to lay Callum down, he paused, then looked at her and said, "Speaking of family, I ran into your mom the other day."

Her cheeks flamed and a queasy sensation hit her stomach. Suddenly, her burning question from the moment she'd gotten this assignment was answered.

She knew exactly why she was here. How this had all come about. Her mother had complained about her to Nash. And even after all these years since the two of them had spoken or had anything to do with each other, he must have felt bad for her.

That wasn't a conversation to be had over caring for triplets—she'd ask him about it when it was just the two of them. "Well, I guess the reporter gets *her* question answered," she said with as much of a smile as she could manage. She was touched by what Nash had done for her, but what she felt most right now was deep embarrassment at what her mother must have said to the point that it had changed his mind about granting an interview. Andrea Watson clearly hadn't held back about what a terrible disappointment Wendy was.

And that had mattered to Nash.

Wendy was aware of something shifting inside her, something tight and uncomfortable suddenly loosening. In that moment, she understood that Nash Dawson was—deep down—still her friend. And one of the little cracks in her heart filled in.

* * *

Nash held Callum and Ryder while Wendy had Dallas in her arms as they went downstairs for the triplets' bottles. The boys smelled heavenly.

And so did Wendy Watson. She'd been so near by the tub that he'd been able to smell her spicy perfume, something sexy. He was surprised he'd noticed it over the scent of the baby soap. But he supposed it was because he couldn't help noticing Wendy herself. He'd seen her several times in town over the years of course, but not up close and personal, like this. She was beautiful. The long red hair, green eyes with the fiery determination that had always drawn him, her delicate features and tall slender body. She looked angelic but she was fierce.

Even now, when she was out of her depth in this strange situation they found themselves in—not the interview part but the triplet part—she was going for it, partaking, not sitting anything out. When he'd been changing Callum and mentioned he always gave them a couple ounces before nap time and bedtime, her eyes had lit up and she said she'd never fed a baby and would love to help.

That was Wendy Watson. Curious. Interested.

But at the moment, she seemed mortified. He could tell by her expression—the same as when she was a kid and embarrassed by something—and the way she bit her lip as they made their way from the bathroom to the kitchen, chatting away to Callum to avoid looking at Nash. She definitely didn't like that her mother had told him her life story—who would?—and he had no doubt

Wendy understood that had been the case. Once the babies were settled for their naps, they'd talk about it.

In the big country kitchen, he set the two babies in the playpen, both immediately grabbing for the squishy stuffed animals inside. "I'll make the bottles and then I'll feed these two and you can feed Callum."

"You can feed two at a time?" she asked, giving Callum a hoist in her arms.

"Oh, yeah. Not at first, trust me. The first few days, I could barely angle one baby against me to feed them. But you know what they say about necessity and invention. I figured it out fast."

Wendy laughed, the earlier flame in her cheeks gone now, he was glad to see. He made the three bottles, told Wendy he'd be back in a jiff and brought the bottles to the coffee table, then headed back to the kitchen.

He picked up Ryder and Dallas. "Ready?" he asked.

"Ready," she said with a smile.

They went into the living room and sat down on the sofa, Wendy beside him with Callum on her lap. He positioned the two babies, the crook of his arms providing a barrier, then wiggled a bit to pick up both bottles. He'd never been ambidextrous until it was necessary, but for the past few months he'd gotten good at feeding two at once. He used to like the idea of paying ardent attention to one a time until he wised up about that when screaming hungry babies put the kibosh on it.

Wendy watched, then positioned Callum similarly and picked up the bottle. She slipped it into his mouth, the baby putting his hands on the bottle. "He can hold it?" she asked in wonder.

"Not quite yet, but they like to touch it while they're drinking."

He saw the way her eyes widened and lit up, her expression filled with awe as she fed Callum. He wondered if she had plans for marriage and motherhood. When they were friends, she had said she wouldn't even think about getting married until she was thirty and established in her career, and a first baby at thirty-two at the earliest. He'd liked her grand plan, found her strong opinions, particularly for herself, very appealing. She knew what she wanted and she went for it.

Like his brother. And good for them. Nash's dreams had always centered on the ranch so he hadn't exactly had to strive much in his life. He admired Wendy. Just like he admired Ethan—too late.

"This is...just beautiful," she said, her eyes soft on Callum.

He smiled, looking down at the babies in his own arms. "When I first brought them home and I was so scared of messing up, this was the part that always calmed me down." He chuckled. "That is once I got the bottle-making down pat. Then I would sit, the boys happily suckling away, and I'd just relax."

She nodded thoughtfully, then tilted her head. "I think the bottle's empty." She pulled it gently away. "Hey, his eyes are fluttering closed."

"Clean and fresh, full belly, dry diaper, warm arms to lay in."

She smiled so sweetly that it brought an image to mind of her at thirteen, just days before their friendship had gone kaput. An article she'd written for the

Bear Ridge Middle School News had gotten a special shout-out from the principal. Nash had gone to her house after school that day, and she'd told her mom about the announcement over the loudspeaker, and Mrs. Dawson had said, "I wish you'd write about farming and ranching issues, Wendy. That's what's important to many in this town and you'd hardly have to spend so much time researching because you *know* farming."

Nash had inwardly shaken his head and came to Wendy's defense, how her article on school start times had helped persuade the town council to push forward all Bear Ridge schools twenty minutes later, allowing students to get more sleep and for start times to better mesh with adult work hours. He'd added how well written the story was, and when he glanced at Wendy, she'd had that same sweet smile. Her mother had even said, "Well, isn't that something," but then had quickly moved on to something else. He'd seen Wendy's face fall. He'd suggested they go get burritos since Thursday were always two-for-one till five o'clock at Margarita's Mexican Café. The sweet smile had come back.

And there it was now. Except Wendy wasn't thirteen anymore. She was all woman. Again, his gaze drifted over her pretty face and sexy body. She was ranch-business casual in dark sleek jeans, a short beige blazer with a ruffled shirt peeking out and cowboy boots. But no matter how beautiful she was, or how happy he was that they were resurrecting their friendship, letting bygones be bygones, not that they'd even brought up the subject, there was no way he'd look at Wendy Watson as anything more than a friend. She had big dreams and those were in far-flung cities. Like Los Angeles or New York. And those places were where he wanted to think of her. He hadn't supported his brother's dreams, but he had a chance to be in Wendy's corner and he was. Whole hog. He would keep his attraction to Wendy to himself.

He wasn't looking to get involved with anyone right now anyway. Nash had done his fair share of dating before he'd taken in the triplets, had some relationships, including a not-serious one he'd ended right after he'd become their legal guardian. All his romances had fallen apart for one reason or another. Most single women in Bear Ridge knew who he was because it was a small town, and his brother's local fame had made Nash particularly "eligible."

He inwardly scowled at the thought of that. He'd always been able to tell right away who was interested in the sheen and who was interested in him, but nothing had ever worked out so...whatever. He was very busy, had his hands full and dating was the furthest thing from his mind.

Anyway, Wendy Watson was here to do a job, then she'd hit the road, and hopefully the article all of Wyoming wanted to read would have her on her way to achieving those dreams. He'd get his old friend back, if just for a little while, and that was worth quite a lot.

Chapter Three

Wendy stood with Nash in front of the three mini cribs in the nursery, staring in amazement at the sleeping Dawson triplets. Her ears still rang a bit with the loudest cries she'd ever heard—from Dallas. Nap time had been *something*. My goodness. Nash did this *every* day? *Twice* a day?

They'd brought the boys upstairs after their bottles, gave them one last diaper change, then settled in the two rocking chairs by the window, Nash holding Callum and Ryder, and Wendy cuddling Dallas. He'd fought sleep like it was his job, his eyes dropping and then popping open as Nash had told a bedtime story. Nash had said he used to read them stories from the books lining the shelves in the nursery, but he couldn't easily hold a book and a baby at the same time, so he just started making up stories about walking, talking sandwiches or bear cubs.

As he'd told his nephews a tale about three bear cub brothers exploring the forest, she'd found herself charmed and moved…and unable to drag her eyes off Nash's handsome face. His love and devotion to these boys was so evident in everything he did.

He'd put droopy-eyed Ryder and Callum in their cribs, a lullaby playing softly from a speaker, the nursery lights dim and soothing. He'd whispered that she could set Dallas in his crib if she'd like. She lit up inside. He'd warned her that Dallas didn't like to miss a thing and could start squawking but eventually he'd tire himself out. Very carefully she brought him over and lowered him in the crib. But the moment Dallas's back had touched the mattress, his eyes popped open and he fussed. They both murmured soothing words, Wendy singing along to the lullaby, which earned her Dallas's droopy-eyed attention for about three seconds before he started full-out crying.

She'd been worried she'd done something wrong, but Nash had assured her Dallas was the fussbudget of the trio. He'd picked up the squawker and gently rocked him, the little eyes closing, but again, the moment his back touched the mattress, the eyes opened and the crying began. That went on for a good ten minutes, but finally Dallas fell asleep.

"Every day, huh?" she whispered to Nash. "You must be so exhausted all the time."

He was looking down at the napping babies, his gaze so full of tenderness. "I've gotten used to it. I've been reading up on tips and tricks to help Dallas self-soothe, so I'll be working on that this week. And my parents or grandmother come over at least once a day to help out with babysitting while I'm out on the ranch or with mealtime or bedtime, but I'd texted them when I saw you get out of your car that I had company and they should rejoice in the break."

She laughed. "Well, I enjoyed myself immensely. I'm glad I got to experience the nitty-gritty of what it's like to take care for the triplets. That'll really help the article."

He tilted his head then, as if he'd just remembered it. The story. The reason she was here.

And *why*.

"Speaking of family," she said, biting her lip, "you, uh, mentioned you ran into my mom?"

He gave her a smile that felt like an arm slung over her shoulder. Exactly what she needed in this moment.

"Let's go have some coffee and I'll fill you in," he said.

"Sounds good." The coffee—not hearing about the ways she'd disappointed her mother. Which she had no doubt included the fact that she was still single at twenty-eight. She couldn't stop thinking about the fact that Nash changing his mind about an interview meant what he'd heard had been a doozy.

He led the way out of the nursery, keeping the door ajar.

She followed him down to the kitchen, a baby monitor on the table. As he went over to the coffee maker on the counter, she stood in front of the beautiful arched window by the table. "I spent a lot of time in this kitchen," she said before she could stop herself. But the memories came fast and suddenly, one after another of her time in this kitchen with his warm, wonderful family. "Your grandmother loved baking. I don't think I've ever had a better chocolate chip cookie."

He smiled and moved over to a covered plate and lifted the lid. "Guess what these are?"

She grinned. "Well, now I have to have one."

"Same here," he said. "Have a seat. Coffee will be ready in thirty seconds." As he pushed a button, he glanced at her. "Something I don't know about you is how you take your coffee. We weren't up to coffee at thirteen."

She smiled. "Light and sweet."

"Another same here."

She felt that rush of butterflies again, though now she wasn't just excited-nervous over seeing Nash Dawson again. She was honest-to-goodness overwhelmed by him, by this...reunion. By everything she was learning about him. Down to them taking their coffee the same way.

He brought over two mugs, hers a yellow one with polka dots. Because he remembered that yellow was her favorite color?

They sat and sipped, nibbled on cookies, which were as good as she remembered.

"So let me guess," Wendy said. "You ran into my mom in the coffee shop. Or worse, the grocery store with neighbors listening to her complain about me."

"Grocery store," he confirmed. "Bread aisle. But it was an off time and not busy. No one was around."

Small miracle. "Let's hear it," she said, taking a long slug of fortifying caffeine.

He also took a sip of coffee as if giving himself a few seconds to reframe just what Andrea Watson had told him. "She mentioned that you were working as an assistant reporter at the *Cheyenne Daily Gazette*."

And when the executive editor of that very newspaper had called, Nash had clearly remembered that fact. From a two-minute conversation with her mother in a grocery store. That in itself was touching. Nash Dawson was clearly the same kind, thoughtful person he'd been before their friendship blew up. "And I'm sure she emphasized *assistant* as she always does. And how all these years later, after *selfishly* leaving the farm for my parents and sister to run, I've gotten nowhere with my pie-in-the-sky dream to be an investigative reporter in a big city."

His gaze was soft on her. He neither confirmed nor denied, but she could practically hear her mother's litany of complaints, see Andrea Watson throwing up her hands in the bread aisle.

"The silver lining is that I found out where you worked," Nash said. "And when the bigwig of that very newspaper called with an interview request a few days afterward, I said yes on the condition that *you* write the story. If I hadn't run into your mom, if she hadn't let loose on me, you wouldn't be sitting here right now. So there's that," he added with a smile.

She was again equally embarrassed and moved. "Why'd you even care?" she blurted out, then wished she hadn't asked. But she wanted to know.

"Because you were once my best friend, Wendy. And I'll be very honest here. I came down hard on my brother about taking off on *us* and shirking his responsibilities to chase his dream to be a bronc-riding champ.

He started in on that very young, and I was always resentful. Well, you know that. And it got worse throughout our teen years. But when he died—" He sucked in a breath and turned away for a second. "When he was suddenly gone, I was so glad he'd followed his heart, gone after what he wanted most, what burned so brightly in him, you know?"

Wendy felt her eyes mist with tears, and her hand went straight to her heart. He clearly had regrets over his relationship with his brother. "Oh, Nash. I know just what you mean."

He gave her something of a nod, and quickly drank his coffee as if he didn't like seeming so vulnerable. "I tried to tell your mother that but she didn't seem to think it was related."

She nodded. "Because your brother *did* achieve his dreams. And I haven't."

Exactly what her mom had said. "It's the trying that matters. I feel very strongly about that." He looked away for a moment, out the window, and she had the feeling he was thinking about Ethan. Remembering something in particular. "Your dad was always your biggest supporter," he said, looking at her again. "Still the case?"

She brightened. "Yup. Thank God. My sister too. Tess runs the farm and loves it. And she likes things her way. She'd probably hate to have to pass things by me as a partner."

He smiled. "I remember how serious she always was about the farm. Remember when we picked tomatoes in her vegetable garden before they were ripe and she went ballistic on us? She was like nine at the time."

Wendy laughed. "She's very serious about Watson Dairy. And she does an amazing job. Plus, Tess makes the most incredible goat cheese." This was easier—talking about the farm and her sister and cheese making. But there was something she needed to say. "Nash, before I forget to thank you because there's so much for us to talk about, *thank you*. Given that you've been saying no to all interviews for the past six months, I'm sure you're not thrilled about the idea of an article."

He sipped his coffee, then put the mug down. "I'm not. I hate the idea of the saddest day of my life, of my orphaned nephews' lives, of my parents' lives, selling newspapers and getting those stupid care emojis on social media links. But I also get that people actually do care about Ethan's legacy. The babies he and Lydia left behind. How they're doing. How we're all doing. I get it. And I suppose it helped that the reporter I said yes to has a personal connection. Even if fifteen years has gone by without us saying a word to each other."

Fifteen years. How was it possible that she felt every bit of those years that had separated them *and* felt so close to him right now at the same time?

She wanted to follow up on what he'd just said, address it, maybe even bring up what had happened all those years ago. But it seemed so far away, silly now when they were adults—especially given Nash's full, busy and complicated life. A silly old humiliation when she was thirteen hardly felt worth mentioning. Especially now that she was here, that he'd done her such a huge favor at his own expense... They'd moved on without even having to bring up the past.

Everything in its time, she told herself. No need to rush anything. She was likely only staying till tomorrow night, once the interview was all done, but there'd be opportunity to bring up old issues before she left. Even if they just acknowledged the past and let it go instantly. She assumed that was how it would play out. Which was fine with her.

"Want to know the only news outlet in Wyoming that didn't hit me up for an interview?" he asked. "The *Bear Ridge Free Weekly*. They ran a beautiful front-page obituary of Ethan *and* Lydia and her parents, even though he was the only one from Bear Ridge originally. But not a single request for an interview to sell tons of advertising space."

She smiled. "Not surprised in the least. That paper gave me my first job as a reporter back in high school. Well, a cub reporter for the People in Town page. The folks over there are the best of the best." Although as a teenager, she'd thought of that after-school job as nothing more than a stepping stone, something to put on her résumé. She hadn't been able to understand why anyone wanted to work there and not the *Brewster County* paper, which had actual paying subscribers. Now she understood that you could combine doing *what* you loved with *where* you loved—which for many people was *home*. She thought the *Bear Ridge Free Weekly* staff had it pretty good.

"Does the *Cheyenne Daily Gazette* have a soul?" he asked on a sigh.

"Well, they *do* have to sell papers—and ad space," she admitted. "But my boss cares. And I know that Executive Editor Allen McCrane, who you spoke to, also cares. They demand integrity, excellence in reporting, solid sources and *heart*. Like my dad always said—I should put my heart and soul into every story I tell, no matter how small."

"I always liked your dad. And I'm glad to hear that about your employer. I still don't like the idea of the article, but I do have a certain comfort level with you as the reporter."

She put her hand on top of his before she could think better of it, then quicky slipped it away. "Tell you what. I'll promise you something. The first person to read the finished article will be *you*. I won't submit it to my editor without your approval. You can cross out words, sentences, full paragraphs."

He held her gaze for a moment. "I'll shake on that," he said, extending his hand.

Once again, the moment they touched, she felt it in her nerve endings. He was too close, too attractive, and there was too much nostalgia between them. She had to squash that.

"Waaah! Waah!"

Saved by a baby.

Nash had an ear tilted toward the stairs. "If I'm not mistaken, that's Callum. Usually not a fussbudget." The crying intensified. "Let's go see what's the matter."

Wendy followed him to the nursery. Callum, in his green pj's, looked very unhappy. Nash picked him up, but he cried harder.

"I'll take him out of the nursery so he doesn't wake up the other two," he said.

She trailed him into the hallway, watching him gently pat Callum's back, whisper soothing words, rock him a bit, but the baby kept crying. Callum pulled at his ear, his little face miserable. He grabbed at his ear again.

"Ohh," Nash whispered. "He might have an ear infection. He's been showing signs the past day or so and OTC pain relievers seem to help but now I think I should take him to his pediatrician. I'll ask my mom or grandmother to watch the other two."

Part of her wanted to go with him, see what that whole experience was like. But a baby's doctor visit for an aching ear was hardly something for a reporter to attend. And though she and Nash were certainly friendly, they weren't exactly *friends*. At the least, she could offer to babysit while he took Callum to the doctor, but how would that be helpful when she had zero experience caring for *one* baby, let alone two?

"Maybe we'd better call it a day," he said, rubbing Callum's back. The little guy had calmed down a bit but was still tugging at his ear. "Start fresh tomorrow once he's on the mend."

She reached up a hand to the tiny back and gave him a pat. "Of course. What time might be good tomorrow for the interview?"

He paused for a moment. "To be honest, Wendy, the idea of you asking me questions and me answering and trying to sound this way or that—I can't. I'd much rather just go about my day with you observing and taking part, like you did this morning. That way, we keep it natural. Questions come up naturally."

She smiled. "I love that idea. Perfect." It really was. It was exactly what her bosses wanted for the article. In-depth. "I'll get out of your way," she said, turning to head toward the stairs. She suddenly felt very much *in* his way. Here he was, responsible for three orphaned babies, he'd finally gotten all three to sleep, and now one was crying and needing his attention.

And she was taking it up with questions about the interview.

"You're hardly in my way," he said. "It's nice to reconnect." But he glanced away then, and it was clear they both needed a break from all this…reconnection. "As a thanks for all you did this morning, why don't you let me make you dinner tomorrow night. We'll spend the day doing what I usually do with the triplets and the ranch, you'll get what you need for the story, and we can give it a proper send it off with my chicken parmigiana."

She grinned, a warmth spreading in her chest. "That used to be my favorite meal."

"I remember."

Tomorrow they'd spend the day together, and she'd be enmeshed in this man's life. It was a little chaotic and definitely busy but full of so much warmth and love and laughter that Wendy's heart, always a little deflated, felt full. She realized with another rush of butterflies that she'd better guard that heart.

Then again, it wasn't like she and Nash could be a couple. Her life was in Cheyenne with "elsewhere" on the horizon. And his was here, rooted in the ranch and family. Given how strongly she felt about her dreams, she doubted she'd develop feelings for Nash all over again.

But she was well aware that she found him incredibly attractive on many levels.

While Nash took Callum to Dr. Vivino, who had indeed diagnosed him with an ear infection and given him a few soothing drops that seemed to work almost instantly, his grandmother babysat Ryder and Dallas.

"Not a peep out of these two in over an hour," Livvy Dawson said when he returned with Callum, who'd conked out during the ride back to the ranch.

His grandmother was sitting in one of the padded rocking chairs by the window in the nursery, the mystery novel she'd been reading on the little round table beside her thermos of tea.

"Thanks again for coming over, Gram," he said as he carefully put Callum in his crib, sending up a silent prayer that he'd stay asleep. He waited a beat. Success. He dropped down next to his grandmother.

She patted his knee. "Never ending, that's for sure."

He smiled. The past month the triplets had all gotten sick with bad colds at the same time, then his mom had caught the bug, who'd given it to his dad. Only Gram and Nash had remained unscathed.

"You're definitely feeling okay today?" he asked, peering at her. She'd felt a little run-down yesterday but let him know early this morning that she was back to herself if he needed help with the late morning nap. He hadn't because he'd known Wendy was coming.

Wendy. She'd been on his mind the past hour and half that he was at the pediatrician's, her face, all they'd talked about, managing to stay in his head despite his focus on Callum. That hadn't escaped his attention and he'd tried to block her, but she kept poking through.

That he was attracted to her was clear. That he couldn't do anything about that was also clear.

"Totally fine," she assured him, her blue eyes, just like his and his father's and Ethan's and the triplets', backing that up. Livvy Dawson had a sparkle about her, as she always did. Her ever-present silver bun had its trademark red clip, and she wore her favorite comfortable jeans with a plaid button-down camp shirt and red sneakers. She looked a lot younger than eighty-one.

His parents, both fifty-six, had had to slow way down the past couple of years because of their health issues, including no longer doing any physical work on the ranch. But his mother still liked to handle the books and his dad was in charge of inventory, which made them happy. Gram was in good health and he was grateful for that but he was always mindful that she was eighty-one.

All three were marvels with the triplets, but Nash didn't like to take advantage of their love and devotion to the babies. His mom and grandmother generally took the morning and afternoon nap shifts—which included lulling them to sleep—so that Nash could be out on the ranch and that added up to a solid five hours a day right there. He had some reliable sitters on call too, neighbors who loved the novelty of babysitting the triplets and often brought a relative to help out. Between the home team and his excellent employees—two hands and a cowboy—he was able to take care of the ranch and the triplets just fine. That was *now* though, when he knew what he was doing. Those first two months he'd been a mess and a wreck.

"So tell me about your reunion with Wendy Watson," Gram said, taking a sip of her tea. "How nice that you two are finally burying the hatchet after all these years. You were the best of friends once."

Right after he'd gotten off the phone with the editor of the *Gazette* yesterday afternoon, he'd loaded up the triplets and wheeled the big stroller down the path to the one-story house his parents and grandmother shared. He'd explained the whole thing, from running into Wendy's mother to the executive editor calling, and the three Dawsons had said they were glad he'd finally come around to an interview. They'd been pestered themselves and had turned down all requests because they knew how Nash felt about it and they'd agreed with him to a degree. But they'd always seen it more from the other side—that folks had adored his brother, the champion from a small Wyoming town with the movie star looks and triplet newborns.

People just want to know those little babies are okay, that you're okay, his grandmother had said months ago when he'd first complained about the nonstop requests.

His mom had nodded. *Of course everyone wants to read about that, how you stepped in and changed your entire life to become guardian to those boys. Yes, we help, but the lion's share of taking care of those babies falls to you, Nash.*

His dad had never been against interviews either. *Sure, the story will sell papers. But that's for a good reason.*

"I have a good feeling about her," Nash said to his gram. "That I can trust her as a reporter, I mean."

His grandmother seemed to be waiting for him to continue and when he glanced out the window instead, she said, "I always thought you two would end up together. We all did."

He certainly never had. He'd been too young before their friendship had ended to care about stuff like that. And after, well, he and Wendy were done for good. "We were always just friends."

"I asked you a few times back then what happened, why she stopped coming around, why the friendship seemed over, but I don't think you ever did give me a straight answer. What *did* happen between you two?"

He let out a sigh as memories of that night came back to him. A living room fifteen years ago. A bunch of newly turned teens at a party. "Spin the bottle gone wrong. We were at one of the first boy-girl parties, someone's birthday, and it was her turn to spin and it landed on me. I thought she'd insist on spinning again, since everyone knew we'd been best friends since preschool. But instead she got up and reached for my hand to go into the make-out closet, and I panicked like the idiot thirteen-year-old I was. I shook off her hand and called out that Wendy should get a do-over. She turned beet red."

His grandmother's eyes widened. "That poor girl had a crush on you."

"And I humiliated her without realizing it. And when we tried to talk about it later that night, it went from bad to worse. And that was it. She felt humiliated. I felt confused and shocked and had no idea what else to say so I clammed up. We never spoke again. Every time we'd pass each other in the halls at school afterward, we'd both just feel so embarrassed that it trumped how much we actually missed each other."

"Aww," Gram said, dropping a hand on his arm. "Well, maybe the two of you are meant to have a second chance. Unless you're still not interested in her that way."

"She's very attractive," he said honestly as Wendy's beautiful face and long red hair and sexy body came to mind. He was interested, all right. "But the last thing I have time for is a relationship. I can't start something right now."

Certainly not with Wendy. There were two huge reasons why.

The first was that her life was elsewhere. In Cheyenne for the meantime but beyond as well. Her long-held dreams for herself were quite possibly about to come true thanks to where this article could lead. And six months from now, a year, she could be in New York City or Los Angeles, at the newspaper she'd been working toward all these years. *She* wasn't available—plain and simple. And starting something under those circumstances would be a huge mistake. One he wouldn't make.

And then there was Nash himself. He could actually *feel* the lack of room in his own heart for anyone else. Before the plane crash that had taken the lives of Ethan, his wife and in-laws, Nash had actually started feeling like he was finally ready to settle down, find a lady to share his life with. He'd been dating someone for a month then, but he'd been aware of a lack of real connection between them. And when he lost his brother, something had closed off inside him. Something in his chest had shrunk, hardened. The grief, the shame and regret at how he'd spoken to Ethan the day before…

All those terrible emotions had settled heavily on and in him the first months afterward. And now it was just a part of him. The past month or so, he'd started thinking about dating again—for the triplets' sakes, yes, but his own too. And because his family thought he should. But the few dates he'd gone on had been a bust. He just wasn't fully present as he sat across from each woman on their coffee or dinner date. He just had too much on his mind. The babies he could talk about, but did women really want to hear him talk about Callum's spitting-up problem or how Dallas cried a lot? Talking about the ranch would have their eyes glazing over after a while. And the only other thing on his mind, weighing very heavily and pushed to the back where he tried so hard not to let it through, was his brother.

His parents, and his grandmother, with whom he'd always been so close, had tried to get him to open up about his grief, but Nash had never said a word about that final conversation with Ethan. They all knew well how he'd felt about his brother shirking his responsibilities to the family ranch, missing important occasions, including his father's surgery last year. And they'd always come to Ethan's defense. *I told Ethan to compete in his event and not just come to sit in the hospital,* his mother had told Nash. *That it would make Dad happier to know Ethan would be on that bronc...* He'd always felt that his brother should have chosen the hospital waiting room over the event. Those types of things had added up, Nash not letting his brother get away with not being there for the family. Like he was any kind of judge and jury.

He hung his head, the guilt weighing heavy.

How could he tell them, even his grandmother, the awful things he'd said to Ethan the day before they'd lost him? Berating Ethan about not coming to Bear Ridge for Thanksgiving last year, missing another big holiday for a rodeo event that would keep him hours from his hometown when it would mean so much to the family to have everyone together.

Ethan had relented as far as having their parents and grandmother babysit the triplets while Ethan, Lydia and her parents would be at the event near the border of Montana. And thank God they hadn't taken the babies with them. Nash had never been so grateful for the fact that they'd been deemed too young for the plane ride.

"The triplets sure could use a mother figure," Livvy Dawson continued. "You used to date a lot but we all noticed you stopped. We were hopeful when you went on that blind date a couple of weeks ago."

He'd run into his mother's and grandmother's hairstylist, who'd stopped him in town with the triplets in their stroller to ask how he was. She'd mentioned that her single niece was a preschool teacher and had triplets in her class this year and could let him know what was in store. She'd handed him her daughter's card with an, *She'll be excited for your call! Such a beauty it's a wonder she's single.* She'd marched off before he could say a word.

He'd figured a date would get him out of the house, out of his head, and they could talk shop—triplets. But it turned out his date had felt pressured into saying yes by her mother and the fact that he'd actually called, given his situation. She was very sorry, she'd said as their dinner had wound down, but she, *Uh, knew what work triplets were, haha, so...* He'd had to laugh and they'd parted with a hug and a *good luck out there.*

"Well, I've been plenty busy, Gram," he said, injecting levity into his voice. He got up and went over to the cribs to remind himself that these little guys were his life now. He owed it to Ethan to be the best uncle—the best father figure—he could be. His focus was here. Not on his love life.

His grandmother got up too and stood beside him, linking her arm through his. "Well, promise me you'll keep an open mind about dating. Love feels so good, Nash."

Did it? He'd been burned a few times. Got his heart broken bad once in his early twenties. And these past six months, his heart felt like a pile of ashes in his chest. He'd loved his brother more than he'd been resentful of him. Nash just hadn't known that until it was too damned late.

He couldn't say anything so he just put his arm around his grandmother's shoulder and looked down at his baby nephews. Loving *them* felt good. That was true.

And that was all he needed right now.

Chapter Four

That afternoon, Wendy sat on top of a log in the baby goat pasture at Watson Dairy, the mama grazing and her two kids being very comical. One was dashing about, jumping every few seconds, and the other was rubbing its white head on a large tree branch on the ground.

Being here, with her sister, watching these hilarious little creatures, was just what she needed. She'd left Nash's house a couple of hours ago and she was still so overwhelmed. Maybe because she'd gone to her parents' house first. When she'd first left the Dawson Brothers Cattle Ranch, she'd needed a little downtime to process her thoughts, all she'd experienced with Nash and the triplets in such a short period of time. But before she'd even pulled out of the drive she'd gotten a text from her mother.

I hear you're in town and stayed over with Tess last night. Not even a call? SMH.

Andrea Dawson was such a user of the phrase *shaking my head* that it had been added to her texting shorthand, along with a sad-face emoji, which punctuated the text.

Wendy had shaken *her* head. And then had driven to the farm to see her parents. Her dad had given her a big hug, her mom listing her complaints about little things needing work on the farm and if only they had an extra set of hands... All before Wendy had even made it up the porch steps.

For the love of God, Andrea, let the gal get in the house, her father had said while shaking his own head, which had earned them both a scowl from her mother.

I could help out while I'm in town, Wendy had said. Which got an immediate *I'm sure you'll be too busy with your big assignment*.

Wendy had closed her eyes, counted to three and told herself to just let it go.

Over turkey sandwiches and iced tea and her mother's excellent homemade potato salad, Wendy filled them in on all that had happened since yesterday afternoon, leaving out why Nash had requested her. Her parents would assume he'd done it for old time's sake, despite the timing. They wouldn't know that Nash had turned down every interview request for the past six months, and her mom would likely figure Nash had already known that Wendy now worked at the *Cheyenne Daily Gazette* through small talk at the coffee shop or around town. Bear Ridge was like that. *Oh, did you hear that Allison Portman moved to Las Vegas to be a showgirl? Did you know that Linc Fielding got his pilot's license?* Even the birth of the Watson Dairy's spring calves and kids had made the rounds of conversation, according to Tess earlier.

Her father had been full of congratulations and a *You're on your way*, then had excused himself to tackle a problem Tess had been having with one of the calves, leaving her and mother alone in the kitchen. Wendy's sandwich sat like a brick in her stomach.

Well, it's good to see you, honey, her mother had said, patting her hand, then getting up to clear the table. Wendy had stood to help, but was told to go see if her dad and sister could use a hand.

Dismissed. There was just too much tension between them, too much built up, said and unsaid, and clearly being in the same room was hard on both. At least her mother was honest enough to almost say so. But if Wendy had hoped that they might be able to get to a better place in their relationship while she was in town, she was clearly wrong.

"I could watch them all day," Wendy said now to her sister, who was doing her rounds on the beautiful Saanen goats, checking all three to make sure they were in good health.

Tess smiled. "They're so adorable. You know Patience, regal mom, and the kids are Joey and Junie. They're just two months old."

Suddenly, Tess's face fell—and then crumpled. She burst into tears, covering her eyes with her hands. Whoa—what was going on?

Wendy leaped up and went over to her. "Tess? What's wrong?"

But her sister just stood there, crying, her shoulders heaving up and down.

Wendy led Tess over to the picnic table near the goat's enclosure. They sat, Tess wiping under her eyes and sniffing.

"Everything okay with the farm?" Wendy asked. She was 99 percent positive the issue wasn't Watson's Dairy or her mother would have made a passive aggressive comment relating that to Wendy's leaving.

Tess nodded. But didn't say anything else. She just stared out at the land, then at the baby goats as is trying to calm herself down.

"Is it Braydon?" Wendy asked—worried. Braydon was Tess's boyfriend of almost a year. His family owned the feedstore in town and Braydon handled the financials. Tess was serious about him and had said a few times that she knew Braydon was The One.

The look on her sister's face confirmed that. "We met for a quick date in the park at lunchtime today to walk his dog, and we passed a young couple with a baby stroller. The dad took the baby out and was showing her the ducks in the pond. It was so sweet. But then Braydon said—" She started crying again.

Uh-oh. What had Braydon said?

"Tess?" she asked gently.

"He said he didn't think he wanted to have children. And then he started to change the subject, but I pressed him, and he said it was better that I know now before we get too serious. I thought we *were* serious, that we'd probably get engaged on our year anniversary."

"Did the subject of kids ever come up when you were first dating?" Wendy asked.

Tess wiped under her eyes and nodded. "On our first date. He said: 'I think you should know I want five kids. Maybe six.' I told him six sounded good to me." She smiled wistfully as if lost in the memory for a moment. "And sometimes we'd joke around about how if we did get married someday and have those six kids, we couldn't use any of my favorite names because I'd used them for the goats." She started crying again.

Oh, no. Wendy's heart ached for her sister. "How did you two leave that conversation?" Wendy asked.

"I asked him how he could have done such a one-eighty—six kids to *none*? And he said he'd been doing a lot of thinking lately and it was just how he'd come to feel. He apologized profusely and said he understood if I dumped him on the spot. I hugged him and asked if he thought he might change his mind back. And he said no." She burst into tears again, covering her face with her hands.

Oh, Tess. Wendy pulled her sister into an embrace and let her cry.

She sniffled, swiping under her eyes. "I've noticed a change in him the past few months. I can't really explain how or why. He just seemed subdued. And any time I'd try to ask him about it, he'd say he just had a lot on his mind. I'd remind him he could talk to me about anything and he'd sort of smile and nod and change the subject. He was always on the quiet side and I knew that it wasn't easy for him to open up. But I could tell he seemed to be going in the opposite direction almost. Like instead of us getting closer, we just sort of stagnated. Now this."

"Do you think you just need to give him a little time?" Wendy asked. "I mean, you clearly have given him time, but now that he's made this definitive statement about kids, maybe you could wait a day or two, and then say you really do need to know for sure because you *want* kids."

Tess nodded. "I can't imagine not being a mom someday, Wendy. I *do* want five kids. I've always said you're gonna be spending a fortune on birthday and Christmas presents for your nieces and nephews." She tried to smile but looked so unhappy and worried.

"Could something have happened to suddenly make him feel this way?" Wendy asked. "Has he gone through anything recently?"

"He has a grandpa who's not doing very well, and I know that's been weighing on him. His grandparents were a big help to his dad raising him after his mom died when he was little. They're very close."

The faces of the three Dawson triplets came to mind. Orphaned at one month old. She bit her lip.

"Well, I can't see going from wanting five or six kids to none unless something got to him," Wendy said. "Hopefully you'll get him to open up and you'll help him through whatever's made him change his mind?"

Tess brightened. "It's all I can do, I guess." She sat for a few moments, staring out at the woods, then at the goats, always good for a smile. Then she glanced at her watch. "Okay, farmwork never ends so luckily I'm too busy to sit and worry." She popped up. "Come help me do my afternoon check on the cows and you can tell me about all your morning with Nash Dawson." Her eyes were full of curiosity, so at least she knew her sister truly wanted to change the subject.

"Well, seems my old crush on him hasn't gone away," Wendy said as they headed toward the pasture where the cows were grazing. "It didn't after we stopped being friends and now its back, fifteen years later. How is that possible?" She shook her head. "Wait. Scratch that. I know how. He's gorgeous. And a really good guy. He takes such good care of his little nephews. He's so devoted to them. It's really something to see, Tess."

Her sister smiled. "And the interview will end up changing your life. Who knows—maybe you two will discover you were always meant to be together, after all."

Wendy shook her head. "Definitely not. I might be in New York or Chicago or LA in a year, living my dream. And anyway, Nash wasn't attracted to me way back when and I doubt he is now. I look the same as I did at thirteen."

Tess smiled. "You mean beautiful?" She slung an arm over Wendy's shoulder. "You two were best friends. That kind of chemistry doesn't disappear."

There *was* something special between them, that was true. Even now, even still. She felt it. An old familiarity, a comfort level, a history. But if Nash Dawson suddenly found her attractive, wouldn't she have felt that? Wouldn't he have looked at her differently? She'd know, given that those signs were all she'd wanted fifteen years ago—and he'd made it clear back then they weren't there for a reason.

She was in Bear Ridge for a work assignment. She'd do a great job, hopefully make some peace with her mom in her spare time, she'd be there for her sister, and then she'd be leaving with her sights set on a big city. A front-page story was a big deal. And the story itself was a big deal. Folks had adored Ethan Dawson, and the heartbreak over his loss, over leaving infant triplets, had really affected people. She'd do Nash and the Dawson babies justice with the story. And then she'd move on.

Her crush on Nash was surely mostly nostalgia. She'd be gone in a few days with her past settled, and when she came home for holidays and birthdays to visit her family, she and Nash could meet at the coffee shop, triplets in tow, and catch up a few times a year. That would be nice.

But she was aware that she'd been unable to stop thinking about Nash Dawson since leaving his ranch today. And that her crush felt like something bigger already.

The next morning at 7:20 a.m., Nash was having a brief meeting in the barn with the ranch hands and cowboy on duty to check in. All was thankfully well this morning. His mom had been watching the triplets for the past forty-five minutes. They tended to sleep until 6:30 a.m. and woke up on cue. He'd been showered and dressed, changed three diapers, got them into fresh pj's, gave Callum his antibiotic for his sore ear and just finished giving Ryder his bottle when his mom arrived. She'd texted a few minutes ago that the triplets were giggling up a storm on their play mats, no fussbudgets, though Ryder didn't love tummy time the way his brothers did.

Wendy was due over at 7:30 a.m. All night he'd been anticipating seeing her again. Looking forward to it more than he'd expected. His immediate plan was for them to have breakfast together. He'd settle the triplets in their high chairs, make him and Wendy an easy meal of bagels and cream cheese, coffee and OJ, get that on the table, and then the two of them could feed the triplets their jarred oatmeal, which they loved. Or maybe he should actually handle the routine on his own, to show her—and the paper's readers—that he was up to the task. He'd fed the trio on his own plenty of times. He'd done bath time and bedtime solo often as well. But he'd never turn down helping hands, and he had no interest in pretending that being the single guardian of three babies was easy.

He thanked his three excellent employees and headed to the house to relieve his mom. He found her and the triplets in the living room, the trio resting in their bouncers side by side as Grandma read them a story about a naughty puppy named Chompers. Granted, his mom was an expressive reader, but the way Callum was laughing every time he heard the word *Chompers*, you'd think he understood what she was staying. They'd noticed that the boys found certain words hilarious. Like *boo-boo*. And *yummy* said in a singsong voice.

Now Dallas was laughing and shaking his rattle.

As always when he came home after being away from the triplets for even a short time, his heart swelled in his chest.

His mother finished up her story, baby laughter all around as she shut the book with a flourish, which had them both laughing too. Infectious. Polly Dawson opened and shut the book again to even louder baby laughter.

The doorbell rang just then. Wendy.

Nash went to the door and the moment he opened it and saw Wendy Watson standing there on the porch, in a Western shirt, jeans and cowboy boots, her long red hair in a low ponytail, he was hit by a yearning. Sexual attraction, yes. But something more that he couldn't put his finger on.

Serious interest. He liked her, pure and simple, he realized with surprise. He could barely drag his eyes off her.

"Wendy Watson!" his mother called, hurrying over to wrap Wendy in a warm hug. "How wonderful to see you. How's your family? The farm?"

That was Polly Dawson, the friendliest person he'd ever known. She was aware he and Wendy hadn't been friends in fifteen years; the subject had briefly come up when his mom mentioned to him that Wendy had sent the family a heartfelt condolence card after the plane crash and how nice of her to think of them.

That was nice of her, he'd said, *but I haven't talked to her in years. Decades.*

That seemed hard to fathom now. The lack of her

in his life all this time. In the first few weeks after he'd lost Ethan, he'd found himself wandering on the ranch, in pain, unsettled, the ache in his chest unbearable. And a few times he'd thought, *It's so stupid that Wendy Watson is alive and well somewhere and not in my life.* The finality of losing his brother had brought up all kinds of thoughts like that. Things he'd taken for granted before had moved to a different list in his head. Keeping in touch had become more important, no matter how busy he was now.

Wendy chatted animatedly with his mother, looking between the two of them as she told them about the baby goats and calves, how well her sister's asparagus and artichokes had done this spring.

"And look at you, Wendy!" his mother said, her eyes shining. "What an impressive young woman. The *Cheyenne Daily Gazette* is a major newspaper—I recently read that they won two Pulitzers the past few years. Tell us all about your exciting job!"

Wendy was beaming as she spoke about the newsroom. Her joy, her ambition, her happiness as she spoke about being a reporter was so evident on her beautiful face, in her voice. She looked at the triplets, her gaze soft. "I met these little charmers yesterday. Ethan, his wife and her parents would be comforted to know that Nash is taking such loving, devoted care of them."

He felt that square in his chest.

His mother beamed. "He is, isn't he. Ethan would be so proud of the job Nash is doing."

Both of them looked at Nash with warm smiles. He didn't know how proud his brother would be of him, given how badly their last conversation had gone. But he was putting everything into raising Ethan's sons. In that, he would not let his brother down.

The way he had with their final phone call.

"Oh, gosh—look at the time," his mom said with a glance at her watch. "I have to get going. Nash, honey, if you need me or Dad later, just give a holler." She gave each triplet a kiss on the head, said a warm goodbye to Wendy, kissed Nash on the cheek and then left.

Wendy's expression seemed wistful. "You've heard me say this before, Nash, but you are so lucky to have a mom like that. Supportive and easygoing and warm."

Without thinking, he reached for her hand and gave it a squeeze. He knew how tense things always were between her and mother. Even something as innocuous as breakfast, how Wendy buttered toast, could result in a comment from Andrea Watson that would set Wendy on edge. The two of them needed to learn how to communicate with each other, what to let go. But that had been the case forever and wouldn't be solved in the few days Wendy was in town.

"Ba!"

They both turned to find Dallas staring at the little dangling mobile above his bouncer.

"What does that mean in baby speak?" Wendy asked with a smile.

"It could mean anything from 'I like the mobile' to 'where is my cereal, slowpoke?'" He turned back to Wendy. "They just had their first tastes of solids the past couple of weeks and made their happiness known."

"I'd love to help feed them," Wendy said. "It would be another first for me."

He tilted his head, as if thinking. "I'll be honest—I was wondering if the article should show me doing the basic routine myself, but then I realized that even though there are plenty of days where I handle feeding or bedtime or bath time on my own, I generally have help, whether from my family or someone stopping by. I can count on one hand the number of times over the past six months that I handled an entire day on my own."

Wendy's stared at him in surprise. "That's amazing, Nash. It's more than amazing—it's beautiful. To have that kind of support and love from those who care about you and these little guys."

He smiled. "Yeah, that's how I see it too. So trust me, if you want to help give them their oatmeal, I will not turn it down. Especially not to make things look different in the article than they really are. Let's go grab the boys and I'll make us breakfast so we can eat as they eat."

She beelined for Callum, who was on the end, and he scooped up Ryder and Dallas and then led the way into the kitchen. Once they were harnessed into their high chairs around the kitchen table, each happily batting on the tray, Nash grabbed the bagels and got two in the toaster oven, then got out the cream cheese. While Wendy was entertaining the boys with a round of peekaboo, which had them rapt and giggling, he quickly made a pot of coffee.

He got the grown-ups' breakfast on the table, then

went to the cabinet for three jars of oatmeal baby cereal and grabbed three little colorful spoons from the jar full of baby utensils. In between bites of their bagels and sips of coffee, they fed the triplets, Ryder turning his head just in time for a glop of oatmeal to land on the side of his mouth. He immediately burst into tears.

"Oh, it's just a little cereal, bud," Nash said, dabbing at the mess with a napkin. "How about a new spoonful?" He fed the baby another spoonful.

"This is the sweetest thing," Wendy said as she held a spoonful to Dallas's mouth. He opened and inside the spoon went. Wendy almost gasped. "I know it must sound nutty to you, but this is so magical."

He nodded, aware of the way his heart lifted at what she'd said. "There's something very special about feeding a baby. Well, you found that out yesterday when you gave Dallas his bottle. Babies are so trusting, so dependent. It makes a person want to do absolutely right by them."

She looked up at him and smiled, her attention immediately taken back by Dallas who was patiently waiting with his little mouth open for the next bite of cereal. But somehow the spoon and Dallas's hand collided and the glop of oatmeal landed right on Wendy's nose.

She burst out laughing. "Is this a good look for me, Dallas?" she asked the baby. She wiped off the cereal and gave him a fresh spoonful. "Rookie mistake," she said to Nash. "Not watching where those tiny hands are."

He smiled. "Yup. Been there, done that. Ryder once

yanked my ear so hard I honestly thought it might have come off."

They laughed and talked and barely ate their own breakfasts, but the jars were eventually empty and it was time for burping. "At almost seven months, it's not always necessary to burp them, especially after solids, but because they're so babbly and laugh a lot, might as well just in case they swallowed some air."

She smiled. "I'm on it. And I dressed for the occasion—to spend a day with three babies. Bring on the spit-up!"

He smiled back but he could feel it fade as his gaze ran across her clothes—the fitted Western shirt with pearl buttons and dark jeans that hugged her curves. Peach-colored socks. He swallowed as he took her in, then quickly looked away so he wouldn't get caught staring. Or admiring. "There's a stack of burp cloths in that metal basket on the far end of the table," he said fast.

She stood and grabbed one, settled it across her chest and shoulder, then unstrapped Dallas's harness. She picked him up, holding him vertically with his head up by her shoulder, and patted his back. Dallas didn't burp though, so she walked a bit around the kitchen, alternating between rubbing and patting. Still no burp. "Maybe you just don't have it in you," she said to Dallas. Except as she went to put him back in the high chair, he started fussing. "Hmm, do you like my arms or do you need to burp? *That* is the question."

Nash smiled. "That is basically always the question."

She gave Dallas one last set of pats and a giant burp

emerged. They laughed and each took one of the remaining triplets. Two more burps followed.

"How about a little playtime, guys?" he said to them, carrying two into the living room and setting them on the play mats. Wendy set down Callum beside his brothers. He brought over a basket of toys and set some out, all three babies reaching for favorites.

Ah, the happy noise of babbling, shaking rattles and baby laughter.

"I could watch them just exist all day," Wendy said, sitting cross-legged on the other side of the play mat. He suddenly wished she was a little closer. He'd been able to smell her spicy perfume before but now he couldn't. "They're fascinating and adorable."

He smiled. "That's how I see it too. I love witnessing them experience something for the first time. Whether they love it or hate it."

"What do they hate?" she asked.

"Bedtime. And none of them likes green beans. In fact, they each prefer a different green vegetable puree. Ryder *loves* spinach. Callum, not so much."

"I have no idea how you keep track of all that in your head. Or do you have a cheat sheet in your pocket? On your phone in your Notes app?"

Nash laughed. "Oh, trust me, I used to. Now, it's all in here," he said, jabbing a thumb toward his head.

"So there are days you handle *everything* on your own?" she asked. "I can't even imagine. Even if all goes perfectly, there's still just the constant need to *watch* them. I mean just plain keeping an eye on three wiggly babies."

He nodded on a chuckle. "I'm much better at the overall care of them than I was even two months ago. I know what to anticipate. Who gets cranky about what. Who's easier to change first. That kind of thing. They've trained me. And they'll keep training me."

She glanced at him, then at the triplets, then back at him. Her mind was working, he could see. About to ask him something he might not like? "I've been wondering something, Nash. If it's too personal a question, I'm sure you'll tell me so. Actually, a couple of somethings. As a reporter *and* as your old friend."

His gut tightened. For a second there, he almost forgot she was a reporter. Wendy Watson was so familiar, even with this beautiful grown-up face. Even with this woman's body. He kept seeing her as his old buddy—who he was clearly very attracted to. He had to remember why she was here.

Still, there was some comfort in still being able to read her. She had the same mannerisms she'd had as a kid.

"I'm glad you added that last part because it reminds me that I need to be careful," he said. "You seem like a kind, genuine person, but as we both know, it's been years since we've talked before yesterday."

Wendy seemed to take that in. "I *am* here to write a story about how the triplets are doing and I do want to cover all the angles, which includes getting basic information. I can assure you though that my heart, mind and soul are with all of *you*—the triplets and the Dawsons, including your family, Nash. I'm an employee of the *Cheyenne Daily Gazette* and I take my position very seriously. But I won't do my job at your expense. You can count on that."

He actually felt his shoulders unknot. He let out a breath, glad she'd said all that. "I know that deep down. Or I wouldn't have brought you here." He hadn't really thought about that until just this moment, but it was true.

One thing he'd learned was that people, at their core, didn't change. Wendy was good people.

"Well, go ahead and ask your questions," he said. "I will absolutely tell you if what you want to know is too personal." He braced himself anyway. There was a lot she could ask.

She nodded. "I'm curious if you have a special someone in your life. Someone who may step into the role of mother figure for the triplets. I think readers will definitely want to know that."

He should have figured she'd ask that since it was hardly going to come up naturally today in the form of a girlfriend popping in He supposed the topic hadn't been on his radar because the subject of dating was far from his mind. "I'm not dating anyone. Between the very heavy grief and the learning curve of taking care of the triplets, I've had a full plate. And now that I'm in a good routine, I'm just focusing on my nephews. But I suppose that one day, I'll probably want to settle down, find that wonderful mother figure for them."

One day in the far future.

She was staring at him. Intently. He wondered what she was thinking. Every now and then she'd pull a tiny notebook from her shirt pocket and the tiny pen clipped to it and she'd jot down what he'd said. Like now. It was a little disconcerting.

"What was the other personal question?" he asked, wanting to end the current topic but now not sure the new one would be any easier.

She seemed a little uncomfortable. "I do wonder why a single, twenty-eight-year-old rancher was named legal guardian of infant triplets instead of other family members." She glanced away for a moment, her expression pained. "Gosh, that was hard to ask, Nash. I want to do my job but I also want to respect your privacy. Your family's privacy. Again, if my questions are too much, just—"

He shook his head. "It's as good and natural a question as the first. Your readers will want to know. Everyone in my life sure did—friends, ranch employees."

He closed his eyes for a second as a memory came to him, and he opened them to blink it away. "I was *second* choice for legal guardian—and trust me, no one ever thought the *first* choice would be necessary let alone the second." He let out a breath as he remembered the day Ethan and Lydia had come over *to talk about something serious*. "Ethan and Lydia sat me down about a month before the triplets were born. They said they'd named legal guardians for the triplets in the event that anything happened to them and were naturally choosing Lydia's parents, who were wonderful and mid-fifties and full of energy. But as a just in case, if it was all right with me, they said, they'd like to put me down as second choice in case something should happen to her folks. My parents and grandmother were both out of the running because of health issues or age. And Lydia was the only child of only children, so there was only me left."

Wendy nodded, her eyes misty and her expression... heavy.

"Ethan said he knew it was a lot to ask but 'hey, the odds of my taking on the triplets were a zillion to one.'" He glanced away and dropped his head back for a second. "Lydia said that she and Ethan had discussed it and they also knew they could trust me to take care of their babies if anything should happen to her parents but 'of course nothing would.' She quipped that they'd better live forever, actually." Nash shook his head and was about to add something but his throat closed up for a second. He let his head drop forward, expelled a breath. "No one ever saw that plane crash coming."

For a moment she just looked at him, and her eyes filled with tears. "I'm so sorry, Nash. I am so, so sorry."

He managed a nod but his heart felt so heavy he could topple forward. "You know that Ethan and I... We didn't always get along. It got worse. When he did ask me if they could put me down as second choice, I was so moved, Wendy. I'd bolted up from my chair and I just hugged him and he hugged me back. We hadn't had a moment like that in *years*."

He closed his eyes for a second and let out another breath, half wishing one of the triplets would require his attention so he could push all these memories—and this subject—away. But the babies remained completely enchanted with their toys and one another.

"But your relationship with Ethan must have been

better since he wanted you to take the triplets as a just-in-case," she said hesitantly.

He knew he didn't have to tell her this was off the record.

But he couldn't get any words out past the lump in his throat. He just shook his head.

"I'm sorry, Nash. God, how I wish we'd still been friends six months ago so I could have been there for you."

He stared at her for a moment, so touched by what she'd said that he still couldn't get words out.

"I haven't told anyone about how bad things were between me and my brother," he finally said. "I was always accusing him of being selfish, only thinking about himself and his career in the spotlight." He shook his head and dropped his head in his hands. He couldn't even bear telling her that he'd done so the very last time he ever spoke to Ethan. The day before died. "My last conversation with him," he choked out. "The day before— It…wasn't good."

He was aware of Wendy coming over and sitting down beside him. She put an arm around him and something inside him just…broke. He pulled her into an embrace, whether needing his old best friend in this moment or just needing a damned hug right now—he wasn't sure.

"I'm so sorry, Nash," she said, tightening her hold. She was quiet for a moment. "Well, it looks like we're friends again," she whispered, "so there's that."

She was so close that he could kiss her. And how he wanted to.

But he couldn't.

He let go of her and gave her something of a smile. "There's that," he repeated. "And that's not nothing," he added with a bit of a laugh. It was something his granddad always used to say. And the fact that she'd said they were friends again filled a crack in his heart.

She gave him a compassionate smile, her eyes still teary, and sat cross-legged again facing the triplets, her attention on the babies.

But something had happened between them, something much more powerful than a kiss. And it shook Nash to his core.

Chapter Five

For the next hour, Wendy enjoyed playtime with the triplets, building a tower out of blocks and then knocking it down, which got the biggest baby laughs she'd ever heard, and telling them a made-up story about the baby goats at the Watson Dairy. But the entire time, she'd been so aware of Nash and all he'd shared. He'd opened up to her and she could tell he hadn't meant to. That was the power of a very old, cherished friendship, even if it had ended long ago. Just like she felt she still knew Nash Dawson, he clearly felt the same way about her. He'd said as much about why he trusted her to write the article.

The moment Nash had come toward her from the barn the day she arrived, she could see the heaviness in his eyes, his expression. Grief. But now she knew it was edged with shame, if that was the right word, over how bad his relationship was with his brother—and had been when he lost Ethan. Maybe she could help with that. How many times had her mother called her selfish and accused her of putting her career before the family business? Just like Nash had done to Ethan.

She tried over this past hour to find some perspective, to let it fill in some holes in how hurtful her mother was. But it was hard. Of course, she felt guilty for leaving the farm to pursue her own interests and goals. She had no doubt Ethan had felt the same way. Wendy wasn't exactly sure in what way she could help Nash find some peace with this but maybe trying would bring *her* a little peace and she could use that newfound perspective to help him.

She carried a lot of anger over her mother's lack of support and digs. It just plain hurt. She could understood her mom's point of view—to a degree. But Wendy had never believed that she was leaving her family high and dry. Her sister loved the farm—Tess's *life* was Watson Dairy. And her parents were healthy and strong and devoted to the place as well. Every month for the past seven years, Wendy had sent her mother 10 percent of her paycheck to help with hiring a farm hand to take her place. The first few years, that hadn't added up to much. But this past year, she'd done better salary-wise. And if this story led to a promotion, she could send even more home.

She was sure that Ethan Dawson had contributed to the family ranch too, not that Dawson Brothers Cattle was struggling the way Watson Dairy could some months. But all that was personal and had nothing to do with the story she'd write.

"Who's ready for their morning nap?" he asked the triplets. "Uncle Nash sure is!" He smiled at them.

Uncle Nash. She supposed he'd always be Uncle Nash to the Dawson boys even two, ten, thirty years from now. As a tribute to the fact that they'd had a father who'd loved them very much and Nash clearly didn't intend to take over that title for himself.

She watched him interact with them, running a soft finger down Callum's cheeks, blowing a soft raspberry on Ryder's belly, which elicited more baby giggles, and then scooping up Dallas to hoist him high in the air.

For the moment, Nash seemed barely aware of her presence and it was so obvious that he loved the triplets with all his heart and soul. And none of it was to impress her or for the article's benefit. It was just true blue, the real Uncle Nash with his nephews.

And close to an hour later, all three babies were finally asleep. Ryder was the holdout this time, fighting his nap until his eyes just couldn't stay open another second. The whole routine, from changing them to telling a story, to settling them in their cribs took a good thirty minutes, then another half hour till all eyes were closed.

"I see what you mean about needing a nap," she said on a chuckle as they left the nursery.

"I'll settle for coffee. You?"

"Absolutely," she said, following him into the kitchen. "You sit. Let me get it."

He smiled and the way it lit up his face stopped her in her tracks for a second. "I'll never turn down the opportunity to sit."

She got the coffee going and found the mugs in the cabinet. "I can imagine how tired you must always be. I guess it just becomes part of things?"

"Yup. I thought I was generally tired before—rancher's hours of being up with the roosters, the physical work, the putting out of mini fires all day. I had no idea what tired was until those three became my responsibility."

"No doubt," she said. She wondered if it would lead him to find that "special someone" sooner rather than later. Even with such good, caring help from family and neighbors and friends, having someone right there beside you, in your home…

She realized with a tightness in her chest that she didn't like the idea of Nash bringing someone into his life. Into his home.

Because *she* liked him. Dammit. She'd known that old crush had stuck around—the minute she'd arrived she felt it lingering. But the feelings swirling inside her now were different. This was no tweenage crush.

When she looked at him, like at this moment, she imagined kissing him. Being held by him—because of passion, not friendship. Being in bed with him. That thought sent tingles down her nerve endings to the point that she felt the zaps in her toes.

Earlier, in the kitchen, she'd even had the momentary thought that he might kiss her. But it must have been in her head, created out of an emotionally intimate moment.

And plain old wishful thinking.

Her burgeoning feelings for him didn't worry her though. It wasn't like anything could happen between them. She *was* leaving in a couple days. And Nash wasn't up for a relationship anyway—he'd said so. She'd keep her grown-up crush to herself. If anything did happen between them while she was here, it would be temporary. Heck, maybe sleeping with Nash

Dawson would satisfy more than just her lust for him; maybe it would take care of that old yearning. She could finally move on, perhaps.

Unless of course she fell madly in love with him.

She almost laughed at herself. That wouldn't happen. Wendy's life was in Cheyenne and then points unknown—but points far away. Nash's life was about three babies and a ranch to run. No one was falling in love here.

But still, she'd definitely keep her feelings to herself. Do her job—and then go.

"Waaah!" came a cry from the baby monitor on the table.

She turned with two mugs of coffee in her hands. She set them down. "I'll go check on the triplets. You relax. You've been up since what, five a.m.?"

"Actually, yes, even though the guys didn't wake up till six thirty. I thought I heard a cry but whoever it was must have soothed himself back to sleep because the nursery was pin-drop quiet. And then I couldn't get back to sleep."

"Lots on your mind?" she asked.

He stared at her for a second. "Yes." He was looking at her so intently that she felt a blush rise to her cheeks. She hurried past him for the stairs. "Be right back—well, I hope!"

She dashed up the stairs, needed to collect herself. Had he been saying something back there? That *she* had been on his mind in the wee hours? The way he'd looked at her as he'd said it...

Could be more of that wishful thinking. A lifetime's worth.

She went into the nursery and beelined for the noisemaker—center crib. Ryder. But the moment she approached and whispered, "Hey, sweetheart," he stopped fussing and his eyes drooped. "Hey, little cowboy, don't you cry," she sang, "Wendy's gonna buy you a butterfly." She peered over and he was asleep again. Amazing.

"He must have really liked those lyrics," came a voice from behind her.

She turned and there was Nash, gazing at her *that way* again.

And this time she didn't think it was just long-held hope to see him look at her with anything other than *good buddy* in his eyes.

"I don't know many lullabies," she said fast, trying to drag her own eyes off his handsome face.

He too glanced away—toward the cribs. Tingles ran up her spine. She was *not* imagining his interest in her. This wasn't long-held wishful thinking. He'd been looking at her like he wanted to kiss her.

And suddenly, it was all she could think about.

"I didn't either," he said. "I mangled a bunch in the first weeks. Now I know them all. I still make them up too though. I liked yours."

She grinned. A little too pleased by *both* compliments—unspoken and otherwise. "And it worked."

"Let's go have that coffee before it gets cold."

She nodded but turned back to the cribs to catch her breath, watching the three Dawson babies sleep, Dallas with an arm up by his head. Ryder's little chest rising up and down in his green pj's. And Callum so peaceful.

She glanced at Nash to see him looking at her again. But this time she couldn't read him. She returned her attention to the babies, too aware of Nash's presence in the room. So close to her.

Stop thinking about him, she told herself. *Especially about kissing him.*

"Gosh, I wish my sister's boyfriend could see this," she said fast to get on a different subject. "How sweet and beautiful and magical babies are." *Oh, darn*, she thought, feeling her eyes widen. She turned to Nash. "I didn't mean to actually say that aloud. My sister told me in confidence."

This was how upside-down the man had her right now.

"Her boyfriend has the same opinion of babies that I used to?" he asked with a smile and turned to head out of the nursery. "That they're all uber-needy, crying poop-machines? I mean, they *are*, but they're much, much more."

Wendy laughed, following him from the room but then quickly frowned. "He actually told her he doesn't think he wants kids, after all. They've been dating for almost a year and I know he's the one for Tess. But he told her that it's only fair to tell her now before they made any life plans."

"And Tess wants kids, I presume," he said as they headed downstairs.

"Five. Maybe even six. Just like he did—he told her that on their first date. But something changed for him, I guess. She said he hasn't seemed himself the past few months but she couldn't get him to open up. I think she's worried that he's just changed his mind about her."

"Aww, sorry to hear this," he said, leading the way into the kitchen for that necessary coffee.

She needed it double now that she'd spoken out of turn about her sister. But it did feel surprisingly good to talk to her old confidant about it. Get his take. Like old times. She knew he was trustworthy with all her secrets. He'd never blabbed a word about her biggest one. About her feelings for him.

"He's a good guy?" he asked, bringing the lukewarm mugs over to the microwave as she dropped down at the table.

"Definitely. You might even know him. Braydon McKey? His family owns the feedstore on Western Road."

"Oh, yeah—I know Braydon. He and his dad and uncle are great. In fact, they were all big fans of Ethan's. I got them free tickets to the rodeo when it came this way last year—boy, did that make their day. Well, if you want to invite your sister and Braydon over for dinner or something, maybe seeing how wonderful the babies are, how happy they make me, will help Braydon rethink his position."

Wendy gasped and stared at him. "That's so nice of you. I'd love to do that."

"Well, how about tomorrow night, then, since we don't know how long you'll be in town."

That meant dinner tonight *and* tomorrow night.

Stop reading into anything, she reminded herself. *If*

he suddenly finds you attractive, that's nice and all—really nice—but this can't go anywhere. The two of you are in very different places with very different needs and wants. But if she could help out her sister...

"Let me text her," she said, pulling out her phone. She glanced up. "Nash, thank you. Really thoughtful."

He brought two steaming mugs of coffee to the table. "Unless of course it backfires and the triplets are demons and he never wants to go near a baby again."

Wendy laughed. "I can vouch for those charmers. Even fussy, they're precious."

He smiled, again his handsome face lighting up, and sipped his coffee.

And without any say so from her, Wendy felt the needle move into the I'm-falling-for-you area of her heart.

Fifteen minutes later, Nash was in his home office going over ranch paperwork while Wendy was texting with her sister in the living room. She'd been here just a couple of hours or so today, but he'd been glad for the break to collect himself. During the morning, he'd find himself just gazing at her and he'd have to pull his attention off her. But what was going on inside him where Wendy Watson was concerned was more than just attraction, more than just lust.

He felt a *connection*—a chemistry and familiarity and excitement that had been missing from his relationships and dates over the years. She drew him like no one else had, even the longer-term relationships where he'd been in serious like but had always been aware of something missing. Something he'd never been able to put his finger on. It was *this*—the intangible connection that he had with Wendy.

She was the wrong woman to have that with though. So once again, nothing could or would come of his interest in her.

There was a knock on the open door and he looked up. She stood there, her face lit up, her green eyes sparkling.

"We have a yes for tomorrow from my sister and her boyfriend!" she said, her delight evident.

He was actually surprised, even though it had been his idea. A guy who'd said he didn't think he wanted children had agreed to dinner at a home with baby triplets? Maybe Braydon did want to see that being a family man was wonderful—or confirm the opposite? Nash wasn't sure. Hopefully his suggestion wouldn't make things worse between the couple. "Great," he said, leaning back in his chair. "What should I make for dinner?"

"You mean what should *I* make?" she asked with a smile. "You have quite enough on your plate, Nash. It's nice enough that you offered, so I'll be the chef."

"No argument from me," he said. "Always appreciate a home-cooked meal I don't make myself."

"I know Tess and Braydon both love pasta. And garlic bread."

"As do I."

Wendy smiled, grabbing her phone from her pocket and tapping some keys. "Aha—my favorite cooking site has a tried-and-true recipe for linguini carbonara, which I know they both love too. Sound good?"

"*Very* good."

"Perfect—the entrée is set. And interestingly, Tess said she was surprised that Braydon responded with an immediate yes—with an exclamation point."

"Maybe because he knows me?" Nash asked. "I'm at the feedstore a couple times a month."

"Ah, that's probably it. Familiarity. And like you said, he was a big fan of Ethan's. The idea of seeing these *particular* triplets might be meaningful to Braydon."

Nash nodded. "I think you're right. I hope the idea doesn't backfire on Tess though. I mean, if Braydon has decided he doesn't want kids and being here confirms that—mini-charmers or not…"

"Yeah, I was thinking about that too. But I guess they should come to terms with how they both feel. If he doesn't want a child when Tess wants a houseful, they should know that and they may decide they need to walk away from each other, no matter how painful that is."

It was both very complicated and simple. Agreeing to have a child when you really didn't want to be a parent just to keep the person you loved sounded like a potential disaster. In that scenario, it was also possible that when their baby came along, Braydon would fall in love with his child and be glad he'd agreed, and all would be well.

Or Tess would agree not to have kids to keep Braydon in her life, and year after year, she'd see her friends' kids getting on the school bus and she'd be deeply sad. Walking away wasn't necessarily the answer. But neither was either of them giving up something they felt so strongly about.

Scratch the simple—it was just plain complicated.

"Speaking of children, want to hear something really dumb?" she asked. "When I was thirteen—before we stopped being friends—I used to think *we'd* get married and have two kids. Twins. A boy and a girl. I even named them."

Her cheeks were suddenly two bright spots of red. His own probably were too.

"Good Lord, did I say that aloud?" she asked, looking everywhere but at him. "I haven't thought about that in years. Now I'm telling *you*?" She shook her head. "Uh, forget I even mentioned that. Thinking about my sister and her hopes dredged it up, I guess."

He stood and came around the desk, leaning on the edge. Wendy was still standing just past the doorway, hands shoved in her pockets now.

"I'm glad you sort of brought up the past, Wendy. I think we should talk about it. We never really got to do that."

She nodded. "Maybe I'll sit," she said, dropping down in a chair in the corner.

He could remember everything that had happened like it was truly yesterday. How she'd run out of the house where the party was—one of the first girl-boy parties. Stupid spin the bottle. She'd been waiting for him to take her hand and lead her to the kiss-closet. But he'd reacted like an idiot. *I can't kiss Wendy Watson!*

She's my buddy! And then he'd made a face that had sealed his fate. *Their* fate—as no longer buddies at all.

He'd been so confused and clueless until she just stood there, tears welling in her eyes before running out of the house. He'd gone after her and found her at the end of the long brick walkway. She'd been crying. He'd just stood there, unsure, unsettled, and nothing came out of his mouth. Finally, she swiped under her eyes and told him that he was an idiot and clearly she had feelings for him—romantic feelings—and that he'd humiliated her in front of everyone.

He'd been so taken aback. Shocked, really. He hadn't known how to handle what she was saying. And he supposed, in that moment, she'd gone from being his best friend to someone he didn't know. That and what had happened at the party had gotten so jumbled in his head that he said all the wrong things. *Oh, come on, you don't like me that way. We're friends, Wendy. That's all we'll ever be. I mean, come on.*

And she'd looked at him, her face crumpling, and she'd run away. He'd followed her, though without the guts to call out to her, to stop her, to try to talk. He'd had no idea what to say, how to fix things. How to get his Wendy back. The Wendy she'd been before that bottle pointed at her.

He'd watched her race into her house, the door shutting. And the next day, at school, when he'd tried to talk to her at her locker, as if nothing was wrong, as if nothing had happened—like a complete idiot—she'd shaken her head at him, said their friendship was over and hurried off.

He'd felt gutted, but he'd been unable to say anything, unable to move and he'd just walked away in the opposite direction, his stomach twisting. Once or twice that week he'd seen her in the halls and had been about to say something, but she'd suddenly notice him and rush away. And that was that. Childhood besties suddenly not in each other's lives at all.

He'd been miserable over it for months.

"I was gutted from losing you as a friend, Wendy. You probably know that though. I'm sorry I handled the whole thing so badly—what I'd said and how I'd said it and being so dopey and immature. I'm so sorry. I don't think I ever did say those words then."

"No, you didn't, actually." She gave him something of a smile. "It was a big loss," she added. "But even when I cried myself to sleep for months, I'd think, at least he knows how you feel, awful as it turned out. At least it's not a secret anymore. Because if you want something, you have to go for it. I went for it that night and lost. But at least I tried, right?" She bit her lip and looked away and he could tell she was remembering that thirteen-year-old.

Oh, Wendy. His heart truly went out to her—to the girl she'd been. He wanted to pull her into a hug. Let her feel how sorry he was in the weight of his arms around her. "I'm very sorry, Wendy. I'm so glad you're here. That we're friends again. I mean, we are, right?"

She gave a bit of a smile but he could see she was emotional, as was he. "Friends."

Relief unknotted his shoulders and some of that heaviness in his limbs lifted. "Good," he said. He got up and held out his arms. She hesitated but then stood and stepped into his embrace.

Damn, that felt good. Like in this moment in time, everything was okay. He wrapped his arms around her, unintentionally taking in that lovely spicy perfume, the feel of her against him causing quite a reaction in his body.

"Well," she said, looking up at him and holding his gaze yet seeming a bit uncomfortable suddenly.

She's feeling what you're feeling, he realized. The attraction. The crack in their past being healed. The knowledge that nothing could happen between them.

She pulled out of the hug. "I'm glad that's settled."

"Me too," he said. But he was very aware that something else seemed to have started. There was more than friendship between them now. He could absolutely feel it in the air around them. "Just out of curiosity," he said before he could stop himself. "What were those names? For our twins?"

Two more spots of pink appeared on Wendy's cheeks. "Okay, remember that I was thirteen at the time. Taylor for the girl, after Taylor Swift. And, uh, for a boy, Nash Junior."

He winced, a quarter touched and mostly very sorry that he'd been so clueless back then. That he hadn't known how she felt about him. She'd clearly felt *a lot*.

"Maybe I'll save Taylor for the Australian shepherd I hope to adopt one day," she said fast. "Looks like a pet will be easier to find than a husband at this rate."

"You're focusing on your career," he said. "As you should be. You're going after your dreams, Wendy. I really admire you for that. The husband, children—that'll come. You'll have it all."

She smiled with a raised eyebrow. "Oh, will I? I'm glad you're so sure. Because the closer I get to thirty, the more even *I* worry. Forget my mother breathing down my neck about it."

"I think you'll make all your dreams come true, Wendy. You have the fire. Just like Ethan did. I know that now. What I didn't understand before is that I stayed right here in Bear Ridge, at the ranch, because that was *my* dream. It was never Ethan's and it didn't have to be. Same with you and Watson Dairy."

He'd been slammed with so many truths, so many realizations, so many epiphanies in those early days and weeks after the plane crash. People, even older brothers, deserved their dreams, deserved to follow them.

"I can't tell you how happy it makes me that I can actually do something to help you with your career," he added. "If this article gets you places you want to go, I'll be ecstatic."

She seemed both moved and unsettled at the same time, an emotion on her face he recognized because he'd felt like that a few times himself today. He wanted to know what she was thinking but understood he shouldn't flat-out ask. Pry. People deserved their privacy.

"Well, you always did believe in me and it's no surprise you do now," she said, her green eyes bright. "Another reason I'm glad to have my old friend back."

Except your old friend didn't want to pull you into

another hug and feel your very sexy body against his. Kiss you—long, hard and passionately. Take you by the hand and rush upstairs to his bedroom...

He blinked the images away. He couldn't think this way about Wendy. *Feel* this way. He'd just told her why too.

So remember that.

Chapter Six

What a day this had been. It was just past 7:00 p.m. and Wendy was still at the ranch, still with Nash and the triplets. She'd gone through their entire routine from breakfast to naps to dinner and bath time and had been so engaged and inspired that she barely noticed the hours slipping by. When the babies had awakened from their morning nap, Nash had suggested taking them out on the ranch in their giant triple stroller so that she could get a tour and see how the place had changed from the last time she'd been here, which had been quite a while.

There had been some changes, such as pastures expanded as the herd had grown, and of course the biggest change was that the Dawson family—his parents and grandmother—now lived in the one-story "foreman's cabin," which looked more like a lovely and cozy guesthouse to Wendy. It was an easy quarter-mile walk down a paved path, wide enough for the triple stroller to fit just fine with Nash behind it and Wendy beside him.

Beside him. That had brought back her wild old thoughts of her and Nash being married with kids some day. Even at thirteen she'd imagined that—investigative journalist, wife, mother. She hadn't talked to Nash about the wife-and-mother part because he'd been the star of those fantasies, so she'd kept the focus on her career aspirations. But at thirteen, that *all* her dreams might come true had seemed like a real possibility. Until of course the night she'd known Nash Dawson would never feel the same way about her.

Reality had descended. And she'd started to wonder if she *could* have everything—if she'd have the career and the family. Or either, let alone both. Her optimism had taken a sad nosedive and never quite came back with that beautiful force.

As they walked the property with the triplets, Wendy had looked up at the bright blue sky, then, at the huge expanse, the occasional fluffy white cloud moving. After all they'd talked about earlier that day, how they'd opened up about their past—that she'd actually told him she'd *named their children*, which made her blush now just recalling it—she'd been glad for the change of scenery. The walk outside. The triplets had enjoyed the walk too, babbling away, giggling at squirrels darting up trees, not a fussy moment during the hour they'd spent on the path.

Nash had said the day would have been perfect for a picnic, but that he'd never be that coordinated to manage that and the triplets so they'd have to settle for lunch at home. Which had been wonderful too. Jarred baby food for the triplets, some of which again landed on her cheek and once on Nash's arm, and turkey and cheese sandwiches for them.

All day, as she'd gone through the triplets' routine,

watching Nash interact with them, talk to them, cuddle them, *love* them, all she could think was that these three babies couldn't have asked for a more dedicated and devoted caregiver. Uncle Nash was doing an amazing job. She'd taken pages of notes, adding to yesterday's. She didn't feel quite ready to sit and write the article yet; she'd like a little more time, both with the Dawsons and her own thoughts.

Now, Wendy sat on the sofa with a sleepy Dallas on her lap. The triplets had had their final bottles. Nash was beside her with Callum and Ryder on his own lap, telling them all a story about a runaway naughty calf named Buckley.

Her phone pinged with a text and she glanced at it on the coffee table. Her boss.

Checking in! All going well?

Wendy would respond later when she was back home at the farm. She wouldn't hold Nash to making dinner for her—not after the long day. And she had no doubt Jenna assumed at 7:00 p.m. that she was at her family's and not still enmeshed with Nash and the triplets.

The text was a good pull into reality. She was here to write a newspaper article. This was a professional visit. She had to push the friendship—and everything else she was feeling—into the background.

The problem was that she was feeling *a lot*. Her crush on Nash had grown bigger with each moment.

And she'd gotten attached to the triplets without even realizing it. They'd just crawled right into her heart.

And if anyone had told Wendy that a sleepy baby leaning against her, her arms snug around the little one, would render her speechless and moved, she'd have thought it impossible. Moved by a baby? Maybe a relative's. But a random baby? Pshaw.

Of course, the triplets were hardly random babies. They were Nash's nephews. His precious charges.

And right now Wendy was aware that there was no place she'd rather be at the moment than right here, on this sofa, this baby on her lap, this gorgeous, kind, thoughtful, dedicated man beside her—two babies on his own lap.

"I was thinking," Nash suddenly said, somewhat hesitantly, she noticed.

She turned to him slightly. *Yes, what are you thinking?* she thought, dying to know.

"If you want to be here for the night routine, to go that in-depth for the article, I have a nice guest room that you're welcome to." He glanced at her and then quickly down at the babies, very gently smoothing their soft brown hair. "I, uh, could take my time making us that dinner I promised for all your help, particularly today."

Her heart truly skipped a beat. She sat very still for a moment, trying not to read anything into that invitation. He'd said it was for the article. An overnight stay would let her experience first-hand what it was like to be woken up in the middle of the night by three babies.

That would absolutely deepen her understanding and enhance her approach to the article.

But it didn't escape her that he didn't want her to leave. And not because he'd like the extra pair of hands. He'd shown her time and again he was fully capable of caring for the triplets on his own. Well-placed playpens and baby seats and bouncers around the house were his extra set of hands. Plus, in a pinch he could always call one of his relatives. He didn't *need* her to stay overnight.

He *wanted* her to stay.

The more she realized it was true, the more her heart soared.

But as her heart lifted, her head *worried*. She had to stop getting excited that Nash might like her—that way. It was all moot. There would not be a romance happening here. There would not be a relationship. She was leaving. He was staying. *You have your sights set on New York or LA. He's not even looking to get romantically involved. He'd made that very clear.*

She bit her lip, not sure if she should say, *It's been a long day and I should get going.* Or stay.

She wanted to stay.

"That's a great idea," she said before she could stop herself. "I would love the overnight perspective." She swallowed as she realized it was a *scary* idea. "I'd love to stay."

That was true.

Forty-five rough minutes later, all three Dawson boys were blessedly asleep. Callum had kicked up a huge fuss, waking up Dallas who'd been uncharacteristically easy to put down tonight. But the shrieks had woken him up and then he got overtired. Only Ryder had remained asleep. Between Nash and Wendy walking around the nursery, singing lullabies, patting backs, rocking gently, both had fallen asleep. Dallas had awoken again the moment his head touched the crib mattress, but Nash gently caressed his forehead and the little eyelids drooped to the point they'd finally closed.

"Long day," he said as they left the nursery. "They'll sleep for a good stretch and one or two or all three may or may not wake up."

She tilted her head. "So the last time you slept through the night was six months ago?"

"You're forgetting my amazing family. My parents and grandmother and I actually took turns waking up the entire first month. I got some decent rest in there. Well, when I wasn't up staring at the ceiling out of pure fear. And other stuff weighing on my mind."

She gave his hand a quick squeeze. She could just picture him, lying in bed, eyes wide open, his entire life changed in an instant—and the pressing sorrow of his relationship with his brother. She was so grateful for his parents and grandmother.

Her mother's face flashed into her mind. If something tragic upended Wendy's life, she knew, without a doubt, that Andrea Watson would be by her side in a heartbeat, doing whatever was necessary to support her. Her mother might not like her, but Andrea Watson did *love* her. Maybe that was why her mom's disappointment in her, her barely veiled comments, hurt so much. Because she knew her mother loved her and would be there for her if Wendy needed her.

I need you now *though*, she thought with a rise of sadness in her chest. *For my everyday life. I want to share what's going on with me. I want to hear what's going on with you. And we're miles apart when we're right in the same town.*

"Hey, you okay?" Nash asked, peering at her.

She blinked. "Yeah. Just thinking about something."

He waited a beat as if he thought she might say what that something was. Nash understood so much about her relationship with her mother and it would be easy to talk to him about it. But the subject had already come up, and her own life wasn't why she was here. *Focus, Wendy.* "Do the triplets get bottles if they awaken?" she asked, getting herself back on track.

Nash nodded and turned to leave the nursery door slightly ajar. "Just for a few more days, then I'll stop that. Their pediatrician said six to seven months is a good time to end the middle-of-the-night feedings. But they may still wake up from habit, not hunger. Apparently I have to teach them some self-soothing techniques."

"Ah, I'm an expert on that when I get insomnia. I have all kinds of eye masks, herbal teas, different takes on counting sheep, sleepy-making podcasts."

"Not me," Nash said as they headed down the hall. "I just tend to lie awake and ruminate on everything I got wrong that day and stare at the ceiling."

"You don't seem to get things wrong, Nash. You're beyond good at this."

He stopped and so she did. He held her gaze and moved a hand to the side of her face with such tenderness that her knees almost gave out. She'd meant what she said and he clearly felt it, saw it in her expression, heard it in her voice. And that it touched him that deeply touched *her*.

He didn't drop his hand. He didn't shift his gaze. He was looking so intently at her and something shifted in her face. In his eyes. What she saw there was *desire*. For her.

She swallowed. Once, him looking at her like that, which fifteen years ago would have been much more PG, was what she'd wanted most in the world. Now, that desire was thrilling but yes—scary. For quite a few reasons.

Maybe her nerves were showing on her face because he suddenly did drop his hand and looked away.

"Let me show you the guest room," he said. "Actually, now that I think about it, it was always the guest room. You used to sleep in there plenty."

Wendy felt herself relax. At least the guest room would be familiar and a little comforting for tonight. "I used to love that room. That window with a view to the big red barn and wrought iron weathervane, the treetops and mountains beyond. I would sit on the big overstuffed chair and stare out at the moon too."

"Chair's still there," he said. He reached out his hand, and she slipped hers into it, barely breathing now. He led the way to the room.

It's a gesture of how meaningful the old friendship was to him, she told herself. The guest room was a lovely reminder of the best buddies they used to be. She had stayed over often back then, particularly when she wanted to avoid her mother. She and Nash would stay up watching movies and eating popcorn and talking about what kind of pets they would get when they had their own places. They'd talk names—Nash liked people names for animals, like Harold for the box turtle he had back then.

Wendy smiled at the memory, but then she felt her cheeks warm at how she'd actually told him she'd named their imaginary children. Their twins. She shook her head at herself. Nash Dawson was way too easy to talk to.

"Here we are," he said at the door, and finally let go of her hand.

She took in a breath. Suddenly she was afraid to let him show her in. Afraid her yearning for him would overwhelm her to the point she'd do something really dumb, like pucker up or something. Or just flat-out kiss him. Given how he'd looked at her just moments ago, he'd likely wrap his arms around her and kiss her back and… "Um, I should go get my overnight bag. I left it in my SUV." Wendy's boss had told her it was wise to keep an overnight bag with a few essentials in her car just in case a story she was following caught her off-guard, and now she was glad she had it since her duffel was at her sister's cabin.

"I'll get it for you," he said with an awkward smile and practically flew down the stairs, which told her he was feeling what she was—serious sexual tension—

and knew doing anything about it would *not* be in their best interests.

Her heart was pounding to the point she was afraid he'd hear the roar even from downstairs. And *know* just how he affected her. She went into the guest room, sucked in a breath and stared at the bed. *Would* she and Nash end up here?

Don't do it, she told herself. *Your life is elsewhere. He doesn't want a relationship. One kiss would derail everything she'd worked so hard for. Because then Nash would become her dream all over again.*

And he'd hurt her all over again.

Nash glanced at his phone on his bedside table. It was 2:12 a.m. His head had been such a jumble earlier that he'd exhausted himself to the point he'd actually fallen asleep around midnight. Now here he was, as usual, staring up at the ceiling. But something else was added to the mix of his regular middle of the night ruminations. Wendy Watson. Who was sleeping in his guest room at this exact moment.

When he'd led her to the room earlier, he'd been so affected by her—everything about her—that he'd been relieved for the five-minute break to grab her duffel from her SUV. The moment he'd gotten outside, he gulped in the fresh Wyoming spring air and then dropped down on the porch step for a few seconds. He'd had to shake the fantasy he'd had of the two of them in that room, on that bed, kissing for the first time. And doing much more.

The air had done him good and he'd gone back inside. He'd made the promised dinner, two steaks on the grill with baked potatoes. They'd sat on the patio with the baby monitor on the table. Wendy had gone into interview mode, one question about life with the triplets after another, keeping them light so that nothing might veer into the personal. She'd said she wanted to focus on the "mundane, everyday" aspect of caring for the babies, making sure she got down the details of schedules and milestones.

It had been the breather they both needed and by the time they finished dinner and checked on Ryder, who'd let out a cry but gone back to sleep almost immediately, he felt in control of himself again.

Being attracted to Wendy was something he could deal with, since he wouldn't act on it. Having *feelings* for her was another story. He'd spent the last six months trying to control his feelings, particularly where his brother was concerned, and he'd learned it was just plain stupid and pointless to attempt it. What was going on inside him would come out regardless. At the most inopportune moments too. Not that he knew how to deal with his unsettling feelings. But he'd also learned that with a life as busy as his was, something would distract him from his thoughts in five seconds, like an employee needing his attention or a triplet with arms reaching up.

And there was nothing like holding a baby against his chest, that sturdy little weight in his arms, the baby-shampoo scent wafting up, to remind him of his blessings.

Wendy had insisted on cleaning up the kitchen since

he'd cooked, but he helped anyway, and then she said she'd head up to the guest room for the night to put her notes together and make some calls. They'd said their good-nights and as he watched her walk up the stairs, he'd wanted to follow her. Just be with her a little more.

There were those *feelings*.

He'd heard her door open and close a couple times, the hall bath's shower running, and he hadn't even tried to stop imagining her naked and glistening, her long red hair damp down her back.

He had *multiple* feelings for the woman.

Now he closed his eyes. He couldn't start something with Wendy—that was a given. He accepted that so he'd just act accordingly. Like a friend. It really did mean so much to him to have her friendship back. So he would just be glad for that and work on mentally moving on from any notion of the two of them in that guest bed. Together.

"Waaah! Waaah!"

Hmm, usually he could differentiate between cries, but was that Dallas or Ryder? Callum tended toward less shrill ones.

He threw off the quilt and headed into the nursery, only to find Wendy had gotten there first. He swallowed at the sight of her in yoga pants and a long T-shirt, both of which clung to her curves.

She was standing at the crib, making soothing sounds and gently rubbing Ryder's forehead again and again, a little trick he'd learned worked fast. She'd must have seen him doing that at some point the past couple of days. The baby had quieted and she turned to leave, her expression showing her surprise at seeing him in the doorway.

For a moment, he was transfixed by the sight of her, by his intense sexual attraction. Every muscle was taut, his heartbeat accelerated, and he couldn't take his eyes off her if he wanted to.

He didn't want to.

She stared at him too. Suddenly, she licked her lips and he watched as if in slow motion, that pink tongue sweeping across her slightly parted mouth. A little bit from nerves, a little bit from being parched, like he was.

"Thanks for taking care of Ryder," he whispered.

He could see her gaze moving from his eyes to his lips. Back up again.

"He went right back to sleep," she said, voice low and husky.

The room was so still, so quiet, and he could just faintly smell her shampoo—his shampoo from the hall bath.

Wendy, Wendy, Wendy, he thought, trying not to let his gaze drop from her face to her sexy form in the long T-shirt and yoga pants. But his eyes drifted down to her full, lush breasts—no bra in the middle of the night. The light gray yoga pants molded to her curves. Her bare feet with the sparkly green polish.

The curtains on the window moved lightly as a beautiful breeze came through the barely open window, and once again the scent of her soap and shampoo reached him. He took her in, how beautiful she was, his Wendy, right here, so close…

He moved toward her and stopped just inches away,

lifting his hand to move an errant strand of red hair from her cheek. Then either she looked up or he looked down but their lips were an inch apart and he could not resist. He leaned forward, eyes open, and she did too, and suddenly his hands were in her hair as he kissed her. Warmly at first, then passionately, those muscles even tauter now.

She kissed him back, her arms snaking around his neck.

The second her cool hands touched his fevered skin, his eyes opened and he stepped back. What the hell did he think he was doing?

"I shouldn't have, Wendy," he said.

She looked at him for a moment. "Given where we are in life, maybe not. But all I know is that I've wanted to do that for a long time."

"And I've wanted to since you arrived at the ranch," he said honestly. "But…"

"But," she repeated without question in her voice. "We both know the buts. Let's just leave it there, okay? I… I'll just say good-night."

He held her gaze and there was a lot in those green eyes. Including confusion.

Dammit. Of course, they couldn't kiss. But they had. And a kiss meant something. To him. To her.

He would not hurt Wendy Watson. He *wouldn't*.

She glanced at him for a split second, then hurried from the room. He heard her bedroom door click shut.

And if he hadn't come to his senses in the middle of that beautiful, amazing kiss? She might have. Or not.

But one hot kiss likely would have led them places that would be hard to come back from.

They could not do this. Could not kiss, let alone anything more.

He owed Wendy Watson. For the way he'd acted in the past. And to protect her dreams now. He would *not* kiss her again. No matter how damned much he wanted to.

Chapter Seven

Wendy woke to birds chirping outside the guest room window. She bolted up in bed, wondering why a triplet's cry or Nash's voice from the nursery or downstairs hadn't awakened her. She grabbed her phone from the bedside table to check the time—7:34 a.m.—and saw that she had a text from Nash.

I have the triplets with me in the barn. Doing some inventory with my dad. Why don't we meet for lunch and see where we are with the interview. N.

She frowned, a funny feeling pulling at her heart, and read the text again... *See where we are with the interview.* As in: How fast can we settle up this thing?

Sounds good, she typed back automatically. How about 1pm at the ranch?

A few seconds later came a thumbs-up.

She bit her lip and laid back down. Even though he'd made the first move, Nash was *very* uncomfortable about what had happened between them last night. She could *feel* that through the screen, in his words.

But that's good, she thought. They were both taking a step back, would have a little time to regroup emotionally from that kiss, and then go right back to being professional. To the interview. To the reason she was here.

Which was not to start something with Nash Dawson. Not to kiss. Not to end up in bed.

Or get her all turned around.

She closed her eyes again—more to let her head clear than to try to go back to sleep. She'd had a fitful night of tossing and turning, despite how comfortable the bed and down pillows and soft comforter were. That kiss had played and replayed in her mind. Just when she'd drift off to sleep, she'd wake up in the dark, still thinking about Nash's lips on hers, his hands in her hair, her arms around his neck.

Once, a very long time ago, all she'd wanted was to kiss Nash Dawson. Actually experiencing it had been overwhelming. She was well aware that she craved Nash with a woman's desire now. *Very* different. Fifteen years ago, her daydreams hadn't gone beyond a kiss on the lips—perhaps the French kiss she'd heard about but had never experienced back then—the feel of his arms around her. Last night, she'd wanted to take his hand and lead him to her bed. But then the other kind of butterflies had taken over and she was grateful he'd stepped back.

Finally getting romantically involved with Nash would be a very old dream come true—one she hadn't even known was still dormant in her heart all this time. But maybe that wasn't true. She *had* known. Those times over the years when she'd come back to Bear

Ridge at holiday time and see him from a distance, across the street or heading into a shop, she'd be overtaken with memories and yearning. She'd tamped those feelings down and quickly made herself move on, but he'd been that special to her, that important. The loss that great. She hadn't moved on from it. She knew that now.

But the big plans she had for herself involved a total focus on her career so that when opportunities arose, she'd be ready at a moment's notice to drop everything and take off for a story or a new city. Much like she'd been free to drive off from Cheyenne to Bear Ridge for a few days. This—researching this story, telling this story—was her only responsibility. Derailing her dreams now, when she was finally on her way, would be self-sabotage.

That Nash Dawson was finally attracted to her fulfilled that old dream—that he'd want to kiss her. That he'd want *her*.

So now you can let it go, she told herself. *You can check off that box.*

Except Wendy was no fool. Nothing about this felt *finished*.

So now what? What was she supposed to do with her attraction? Her burning interest in him?

You and Nash can't be a thing. That's all you need to know.

That made sense. So with those words echoing in her head, Wendy got out of bed and took a shower, spending a bit more time under the hot spray than she might if Nash had been alone with the triplets and could use some help.

Wendy got dressed and dried her hair. There was something else weighing on her mind and right now she had a few hours to deal with it.

She grabbed her phone and texted her mother.

Thought I'd come help out right now and visit with you. Good timing?

She waited, bracing herself for a possibly snide comment and a We always need help, so of course.

Great timing, her mom wrote. Come right over. Dad baked cranberry muffins.

Huh. Nothing snide there. Quite nice, actually. Suddenly Wendy felt better all around. She knew she and her mom wouldn't fix their relationship in a few hours while feeding the herd or mucking out stalls. But they could start.

She grabbed her duffel and headed out, but instead of turning left for the stairs, she found herself making a right—for the nursery.

Huh. She knew the room would be empty, so she wasn't quite sure why she'd taken the detour. Sunlight filtered in through the slatted wooden blinds onto the big round rug in pale blues and greens, stars and moons decorating the border. The three mini cribs were empty.

Wendy stood there staring down at the little mattresses with their various pastel-colored animals and crib bumpers. How she wished Dallas, Ryder and Callum were kicking up their legs and giggling, waiting to be picked up.

By her.

She missed them, she realized.

And she missed Nash.

She moved to the window and stood to the right so that she could make out the barn down the path. He was in there with the triplets. *With a piece of my heart*, she also realized, a lump forming in her throat.

Suddenly, she felt so far away.

What is going on with me? she wondered, dropping down on the glider chair. *You have feelings for Nash, and of course the triplets have wormed their adorable way into your heart. You've spent a lot of time with them the past couple of days. Nash kissed you last night.*

Of course, she was feeling...something big.

She got up, that unsettled feeling lodged in her chest, and hurried out. A visit with her mom would quickly get her back on track. Andrea Watson would say some disparaging things about Wendy's career—or lack thereof, in her mother's way of thinking—and Wendy's defense of herself would remind her of who she was, why she was here—and clear her mind. *You know what you want*, she told herself as she headed out to her SUV.

Except she sat there, not starting the ignition, for a good long moment. Instead, she just kept looking in the rearview mirror at the barn—where Nash and the triplets were.

The first person Wendy saw when she arrived at

Watson Dairy was her sister, about to head into the barn. Given the time, 8:35 a.m., Tess was headed for stall-mucking duty while the cows, milked and fed, were grazing in the surrounding pastures. Wendy might have been gone for seven years, but the routine at the farm hadn't changed since childhood when Wendy and Tess had early morning chores. Even as a little kid—five, six, seven—Wendy had always groaned at the idea of her barn duties, wishing instead she could sneak up to a hay bale with a chapter book.

Her sister turned at the sound of the approaching car and waved. With her long wavy strawberry blond hair in a topknot, Tess's face was even more visible—including the strain in her expression. No doubt her sister was thinking about her boyfriend and the recent revelation that he didn't want children.

Tess waited in front of the barn while Wendy parked. "I'm glad you're here. Just the sight of you is reminding me of tonight and that maybe Braydon will change his mind about not wanting kids." She paused and frowned. "Unless you're here because you had to get away from screaming triplets who will confirm his worst fears?"

Wendy hadn't been wrong about what was on her sister's mind right now. "No worries there," she assured Tess. "I woke up this morning to birds chirping an hour ago. I didn't hear a peep out of the babies. Nash had them out of the house and in the barn to do inventory with his dad before I even opened my eyes."

Tess brightened. "Well, that gives me hope. Maybe they'll be on their best behavior tonight for dinner and charm the socks off Braydon. Maybe he'll even hope for multiples." She smiled, but it faded fast. Her sister was truly worried.

Dinner at the Dawson house could change everything for the couple. At twenty-eight, Wendy hadn't felt the slightest warming from baby fever until she spent a little time with the triplets. If Braydon was having negative feelings about kids to the point that he told his serious girlfriend he'd changed his mind about having a family, it was truly possible that an evening with the trio would show him how wonderful, how special, how enchanting babies were. Holding a baby, feeding a baby, cuddling a baby—Wendy had felt the cells in her body change. How could Braydon not be affected? Yes, tonight could change things for him—and his and Tess's relationship.

Now it was Wendy's turn to frown. There *would* be a dinner, right? She was 99 percent sure of that. That morning text from Nash had her wondering though. From the sounds of it, he wanted to wrap up the interview later today. The Nash she knew would not change his own mind about the dinner plans because he was uncomfortable that he'd made a move—and that she'd kissed him back very, very passionately. He wouldn't do that to Tess after what Wendy had told him about the situation. Dinner was still a go—Wendy was sure now.

What she wasn't so sure of was where she'd be spending the night. Probably not the guest room down the hall from Nash's bedroom.

Maybe she'd be sleeping right here at the farm. Writing her article from her old childhood bedroom in the main house, long a guest room itself. Often, during very busy stretches at the farm, her parents would hire on a temporary farm hand and they'd be invited to stay in the guest room. Wendy would hear all about that from her mother. *Isn't it ridiculous that an almost-stranger is sleeping in your old room, doing the job you'd be doing if you lived here and worked here?* Andrea Watson would add a disappointed shake of her head—Wendy could see that move even if the conversation was over the phone.

She blinked to clear her thoughts, but all she could see was Nash's face. His lips, leaning toward hers, the tingling in every nerve ending in her body. Her anticipation, the *excitement*. And then the feel of his mouth on hers, warm and delicious, asking more with each second—until he stepped back anyway.

Tess linked her arm through hers and stared at her. "Hey, what's got you a million miles away? Everything okay?"

Wendy nodded fast. "We're all set for tonight. It's just that..." She dropped her head back and let out a sigh.

"Just that what?" Tess prodded.

Wendy looked for anyone in hearing distance, like her parents, but luckily only the cows were around. She led her sister into the barn and stopped just inside. "Nash kissed me last night. *Kissed* me–kissed me." She explained about how they'd opened up to each other, how they felt like true friends again. Then about being awakened in the middle of the night by a baby's cry. Going into the nursery and standing over the crib. Turning around to find Nash there. Staring at her. With everything she'd ever wanted to see in his eyes. *Lust*. And then how he'd pulled away.

"Wow," Tess said, her green eyes wide and gleaming. Wendy could clearly see that her sister liked the intriguing turn of events.

So do I...mostly.

Her head a jumble, Wendy headed over to the storage locker to get out gloves and a rake. Tess did the same and they got to work, and Wendy could see her sister's mind turning.

"And he pulled away because...?" Tess asked, moving a large clump of straw. "What am I missing?"

"I told you why Nash agreed to the article in the first place, right?" Wendy asked. "Because Mom complained up a storm about me. That I put my career ahead of the family business. That I cared more about my own dreams than the farm. Well, that's exactly what Nash had accused his brother of doing for years. Pursuing his dream to be a champion bronc rider instead of helping out at the Dawson Brothers Cattle Ranch. Not showing up for this or that. Putting himself first."

Tess had stopped raking and was staring at Wendy. "Oh, wow, I had no idea."

Wendy nodded and sucked in a breath. "The day before the accident that took the lives of his brother, sister-in-law and her parents, he had a conversation with Ethan that didn't go well." She closed her eyes for a second as her heart squeezed with how much that had to hurt Nash.

Tess gasped. "Oh, no."

"Nash clearly feels terrible about it. I have a feeling it was about Ethan not having much to do with the ranch. Nash told me he realized that he should have supported his brother and his goals for himself. That people have to go after their dreams."

Tears misting her sister's eyes. "Because Nash understood that life can be short," Tess said. "That anything can happen. Oh, Wendy."

Wendy felt her own eyes fill with tears. "He's haunted by it. He can't take it back, you know? And suddenly Mom comes up to him in the bread aisle at Bear Ridge Grocery, telling him what a selfish daughter I am, and it triggered something in him. So here I am, with this unexpected opportunity to get somewhere in my career finally. But my going after my dream is important to him. Getting romantically involved would throw a monkey wrench into my plans. And his own."

Tess tilted her head. "His own?"

"To heal. To make peace with his last conversation with his brother. To help someone else—his old best friend—achieve her dreams. To be the best father figure he can be to his little nephews. To one day be open to finding a great mom for them."

As the words left her mouth, Wendy burst into tears.

Tess threw down her rake and knocked Wendy's from hers, then grabbed both her hands. "Oh, my God, Wendy, you've fallen for him—for *them*. Nash *and* the triplets."

Oh, boy, had she. "I wasn't supposed to. I didn't mean to. But…you know how crazy about Nash I was at thirteen. He's everything I ever wanted, Tess. And he happens to be a rancher—very much rooted to Bear

Ridge—and the legal guardian, father essentially, of his baby triplet nephews. And somehow, those little rug rats have managed to get in here," she added, patting her chest. "When they were all gone this morning, just down the path in the barn, I actually missed them. All of them. I felt such a yearning to be with them."

"So maybe your dream has evolved, Wendy," her sister said gently.

"But I want to be an investigative journalist. I want to move to New York City or Chicago or LA. I want to tell breaking stories. I've wanted that my whole life. I've worked toward it my whole life."

"And you've wanted Nash your whole life too," Tess said softly.

Wendy stared hard at her sister and bit her lip.

Suddenly, the barn door swung open. Andrea Watson stood there, looking happier at the sight of her older daughter than Wendy had seen her in years.

"Sorry to have eavesdropped," her mother said, the gleam in her eyes making clear she wasn't really sorry, "but I heard you two talking as I approached the barn and... Wendy, this is *my* dream come true! You'll move back to Bear Ridge, be back where you belong, marry that wonderful Nash Dawson, be a mother to those sweet triplets and help out here. We can work out a schedule and—"

Wendy frowned, her chest squeezing. "Mom, if you heard everything, you heard the part about how I've been working toward being a big-city journalist my whole life. I'm finally on my way—thanks to Nash caring about me even though we weren't even friends when you two had your chat."

If her mother felt the slightest bit bad or guilty for complaining bitterly about her to Nash, it didn't show. Then again, what she'd said to Nash wasn't anything she hadn't said right to Wendy's face. Many times.

Except her mother's smile did fade. "Let me tell you something, Wendy. Nash Dawson caring that much about you isn't something to take lightly—or throw away for New York or LA. For a breaking news story. Love—especially with someone with that much history from your past—is *everything*. Should be everything." Her chin lifted as if daring Wendy to disagree.

I thought the family business should be everything, she wanted to shout. But she'd never disrespected her parents and she wouldn't start now. She could speak her mind without being sarcastic.

"Mom," Tess said, "Wendy needs to figure out how she feels and go from there. We can't tell her what's important to her—that's got to come from her. From in here," she added, patting her own chest like Wendy had done a few moments ago. "If achieving her career dreams is where she is right now, then we should support that. If she's in love and wants to stay in Bear Ridge, then we should support that."

Wendy could have clapped. *Thank you, Tess*. She sent her sister a look of appreciation.

Not that Wendy had said anything about staying in Bear Ridge—or being in love with Nash Dawson. Yes, her crush had come roaring back but—

What you felt for Nash as a twelve- and thirteen-

year-old girl was hardly a crush. He was never just a boy she'd thought was super cute and had barely known; he'd been her best friend for years.

And what she felt now wasn't just *like*. Or interest. Her feelings went deep. And came with complications.

Andrea's eyes narrowed at her younger daughter. "Sometimes people need guidance. Wendy is all over the place right now."

Wendy bit back her sigh. "I wouldn't say that. I've been very focused, Mom. Except *now*, something's come into my life that I didn't expect."

"And it sounds like Nash feels very strongly that Wendy achieve her goals," Tess said, picking up the rakes. "Apparently he didn't realize how important it was to support someone going after their dream until his brother died. Nash is not going to stand in Wendy's way of moving to New York or LA and becoming an investigative journalist at a major newspaper."

Her mother full-out frowned. "Well, if he loves her, then of course he will!"

Tess raised an eyebrow. "Um, that's kind of backward, Mom."

Andrea Watson threw up her hands. "The two of you are impossible."

Wendy smiled at her sister and reached out a hand to squeeze her mom's. Her mother gave something of a scowl but pulled Wendy into a hug.

"I want you to be happy, Wendy," her mom said. "Of course I do. But I think love is the answer. Not New York City. Not an *article*. Nothing is bigger than love."

Wendy was so surprised by the hug and the *I want*

you to be happy that she had a delayed reaction to the second part. It was like cold water trickled on top of her head. If her mother really meant that, then why didn't her aspirations mean anything to Andrea Watson? Why didn't she see Wendy's dream as just as important—if not *more* important—than finding a husband or coming home?

Wendy had always been expected to call home on Sundays and it was rare that her mother wouldn't throw in a few zingers about returning to Bear Ridge permanently. Wendy would be telling her mother about the story she was working on for the paper, and all she'd get back was: *When are you coming home for good? Dad and I can build you a cozy cabin... You can be in charge of the goats. I know you've always liked the idea of learning how to make cheese. You and Tess could finally focus on that part of the business...*

Wendy had been standing up for herself for years but when it came right down it, the arguments always went off on tangents when she wanted just one thing from her mom.

To be accepted for who she was.

She stepped back and cleared her throat, then reached for one of the rakes her sister held.

"I'll go check on the herd," her mother said, peering at Wendy as if trying to determine if she'd gotten through to her daughter at all. "Just think about what I'm saying." With that, she headed out.

Wendy let out one heck of an internal sigh. She was about to ask her sister what she thought when she noticed Tess seemed a million miles away, her expression full of questions and confusion. The conversation had clearly gotten Tess thinking about what was going on with her and Braydon. She *knew* her sister. She could see the questions banging around in Tess's head. *If I really loved Braydon, wouldn't I move forward in the relationship even if it meant we wouldn't have children? But if he really loved me, wouldn't he agree to have at least one kid?*

When a person fervently wanted two opposing things at once…

Wendy resumed mucking out the stall. She'd always believed there were times you had to follow your heart—and times you had to follow your head. And if you were smart about things, about what was really going on with yourself, with whatever the situation was, you'd make the right choice, the right decision. You'd just know what to do—your gut would tell you.

Right now though, her head and heart were *both* in each camp. And her gut wasn't saying a word.

Chapter Eight

At 1:00 p.m. on the dot, the doorbell rang. The sight of Wendy, the woman he'd kissed in the middle of the night, had him off-kilter all over again. It wasn't just the hot kiss that had him wanting more of her. Or how she looked in her sexy jeans and fitted button-down shirt, a hint of lacy camisole peeking from underneath. It was Wendy herself—smart, focused, warm, funny, kind Wendy Watson, with whom he'd shared so much of his childhood. He barely had a memory before the age of thirteen that didn't include her. He wanted to wrap her in his arms, just hold her. But he couldn't of course.

Hugs were out. Like kisses. They were gateway drugs. Any touch, bodily contact, would be too much.

And it wasn't just old history that drew him. It was recent history. The very intense past few days.

"I come bearing BLTs and fries," she said, holding up a brown paper bag with handles from the Bear Ridge Diner.

Despite her smile and light tone, he could see her assessing the situation, his expression, his body language, where things might stand between them. The reporter investigating her own personal life, which now included him because of that kiss.

If he thought they could ignore the kiss, just move on from it, he'd been way off. They would have to talk about it.

He smiled back. "My stomach thanks you. I'm starving."

Her returned smile went straight inside him. That bit of an icebreaker helped the tension, and he stepped back to let her in.

"The triplets are still napping, so we can eat in peace," he said, leading the way to the sofa.

She set down the bag on the coffee table, then sat and shifted over the big bowl of shells to make room for the food. Not looking at him. She was uncomfortable and he understood why. He'd initiated that kiss, then stopped it, then disappeared with the triplets this morning before she'd even awakened. He'd said a lot by barely saying anything at all.

"I'll get us iced tea," he said, disappearing into the kitchen. He could use a minute to figure out exactly what to say. He'd already made a promise to himself that he wouldn't hurt her. And the way she'd kissed him back meant that no matter what he said about the fact that there couldn't be anything between them, it could hurt her. Even if the reason behind it was to protect her—her dreams and goals.

He spent longer than necessary getting the bottles of peach iced tea from the fridge and two glasses. When he returned to the living room, she'd set out both their sandwiches, the fries between them. And he was no closer to the right words.

"I know we're having lunch right now, but I need to know—are we still on for dinner?" she asked, swiping a fry through the little container of ketchup. Again, she asked so casually, glancing at him briefly before returning her attention to the fries.

He hated that he had her off-kilter. All his fault. Instead of enabling her to focus on the job she was here to do, he'd let his feelings for her get the better of him. He couldn't screw up again.

And he hadn't forgotten about the dinner, their plans for tonight. He'd thought about it all morning—and he'd been well aware, as he was now, that he was relieved she couldn't just leave after lunch, after they wrapped up the interview. He assumed she had what she needed to write a good, thorough article at this point. He had to get his head on straight about Wendy. If she was ready to write the story, then of course she should leave. He should want that. Not be glad he'd have another couple of hours with her tonight. "We're definitely on for tonight," he said. "This is a very important dinner. We have to unscare a guy."

Actually, this was good. Between finishing up the interview and preparing for tonight—working on another couple's relationship—there would be no time to focus on what had happened between them last night. And what was very much in the air.

She turned to him with a smile. "Huh. I wonder if that's all it is. Maybe he *is* just suddenly scared about next steps—getting engaged, starting a family. Maybe it all just seemed like a lot and it came out as I don't want to do this. I hadn't thought of it that way until just now."

Nash nodded and took a big bite of his BLT, his appetite back now that the subject was firmly not on them. *Mmm, delicious*, he thought, as always from the diner in town. "Should I be honest about something? I don't want to scare *you* though."

Wendy stared at him and put down the half of the sandwich she was about to bite into. "Always be honest. Scary or not."

Always be honest. He tucked that away. "When the triplets were born," he said, "my parents and grandmother and I drove down to Cheyenne to meet our new family members. The first one I held, the first *baby* I ever held, was Dallas. I was thunderstruck. So moved—by how tiny he was, that this five-pound human being was cradled right against me, that he was life itself, and I had to sit down because I was in such a state of wonder. Over a *baby*. I'd never experienced anything like that."

"Aww," she said with a soft smile "But that's beautiful. That's not scary."

He took a drink of his iced tea. "Well, after a couple days, I headed back to Bear Ridge since my parents and Gram were staying for a few days to help out, and I needed to take care of the ranch. And on the way back, I was thinking, wow, that was *a lot*. At least one of the triplets was crying at all times. They needed something *constantly*—sometimes all three in the same moment. I'd never seen so many diapers in my life and I was there for *two* days. And believe me when I say I'd never heard some of those strange sounds those itty-bitty creatures made, and I'm a *rancher*."

Wendy laughed. "Newborns times three, yup. I can imagine it all."

"Here's the honest part—as I was driving home, I was so relieved to be going back to the quiet ranch—and that's with a rooster crowing at five thirty every morning." He shook his head, unable to even remember that guy—the guy he'd been who'd felt that way. "Two days with the triplets made it loud and clear to me that I was nowhere near ready for parenthood. Even *one* baby."

She pointed a fry at him. "But you didn't have to be. Then," she added, popping it into her mouth. "And neither does Braydon—now. Just because they get engaged or married doesn't mean they have to have a baby soon after. They're twenty-five years old. The problem is Braydon saying he doesn't want kids *at all*. That kind of definitive statement."

Nash nodded. "True. I'm just saying I hope whatever very negative association with babies or children that got in his head won't be magnified by the triplets acting like the babies they are. If they're super fussy or suddenly have three explosive diapers while Tess and Braydon are over."

Wendy wrinkled her nose. "I do wonder what got in his head." She bit her lip and looked out the window for a moment, then brightened. "I think the babies will get whatever it was *out* of him though. They're too adorable, too fun and full of life—the very word you used—for that not to happen." She bit into her sandwich.

He swiped a fry in ketchup. "That's what I'm hoping. I guess I brought it up just because I do think you should be prepared for anything to happen tonight. I'd hate for your hopes and expectations for tonight to get dashed."

Like his after that kiss. Doomed from the start.

Now he was thinking about it again. Giving in to his attraction for Wendy in that unguarded moment. Then realizing immediately it couldn't be. That he wouldn't let a new romance between them stick a wedge into her plans for herself. He was so proud of who she was, of her goals. He wanted her to go off and shoot for the stars.

Like Ethan had. And this time around, he'd champion Wendy in his brother's memory. Maybe it would help him deal with some of the guilt.

He sucked in a breath and quickly took another bite of his sandwich so he wouldn't get all emotional. But instead of thinking about how good the bacon was, how tangy the mayo, his mind drifted upstairs. To the babies in their cribs, napping peacefully. Those boys had had his complete heart, mind and soul from the moment he understood, in a daze, that he was responsible for them. He would focus on them, not his feelings, not his attraction, not *romance*.

"It's very possible that Braydon will be totally charmed by the triplets," he tried to assure Wendy, his heart so full of love for the triplets that he suddenly couldn't imagine anyone not being enchanted. "Maybe he'll hold one of them tonight and be amazed like I was. He'll likely just focus on the idea of one baby anyway—unless multiples run in the family and there's a strong possibility he'll get two or three at once."

She slightly gulped. "Hmm, multiples don't run on our side. And I don't think Tess ever mentioned twins or triplets in Braydon's family."

He lifted his iced tea and held it out toward her. "Then, let's hope for the best." He smiled, recalling how shocked—and happy—Ethan had been when he found out their family would be blessed by triplets. Multiples were common on his wife's side. He won't be overwhelmed by three babies because he'll only be thinking *one*—to start."

She grinned and clinked her bottle with this. And he could barely drag his eyes off her beautiful face. "*To start.* I like those words." She lifted her glass to the room and said, "I'm trying, Tess. Hold on."

He smiled at how important it was to her to help her sister. But then the words she'd uttered seconds ago echoed in his head and he felt a frown tugging at his mouth. *To start, to start, to start.*

He and Wendy couldn't start. Period.

"I envy how close you and your sister are," he said. "I wish I'd been closer to Ethan. But I was too busy being critical." He shook his head as the familiar hot rush of shame hit him in the stomach. "I was so focused on what he *wasn't* doing for the family that I never thought about who he was." His stomach twisted, his appetite gone. As his brother's face floated into his mind, then the triplets, one by one, he said, "If those babies grow up knowing that even though they're triplets, even though they're Dawsons, even though they're heirs to the Dawson Brothers Cattle Ranch, they're first and foremost *individuals*, I'll consider my job well done."

Wendy brought a hand to her heart. "Yes, yes, a thousand times yes." She was quiet for a moment. "Want to know what I wish?" she asked, her expression suddenly pained.

He nodded, looking at her intently.

"I wish my mom knew how much I loved her. How important she is to me. How important the family is to me. I wish she understood like you do."

He gave her hand a squeeze, his heart going out to her. "Dreams—even those that take someone away from the family or the family business—should not only be validated but celebrated. I know that now. But six months ago, I didn't. I think your mom will come around, Wendy."

"I don't know about that. I know that she loves me. I just don't think she likes me very much. But I've always felt that way."

He knew how painful that had always been for her. "I know. And that's really rough." His gut ached as he suddenly realized that Ethan must have felt that same way. That his own brother didn't like him. He shook his head again, wishing he could turn back time like Superman, undo, do-*over*. "I hate that Ethan probably felt that same way. That I didn't like him. That I didn't think he cared about us when of course he did. He loved us as much as he loved being a bronc rider. I wish I'd known that six months ago." He stared down at the coffee table, his chest tightening now. He turned to Wendy. "And I wish things were different between you and your mother. I wish she knew what I was too late understanding."

"Nash," she whispered and turned to him, linking an arm through his.

He couldn't stop himself; he pulled her into a hug. He felt her melt against him and though his head said to let her go, he held her tighter. Right now, above all else, she needed this. She needed him. And he'd be there for her.

And dammit, he needed this too.

He moved a silky strand of long red hair that had fallen against her face. Her skin was so soft. He loved the feel of her against him, in his arms. The hug was probably going on longer than it should but he never wanted to let her go.

"About that kiss," she whispered. "Maybe we need to talk about it."

It took some doing to pull out of the embrace and sit back a bit. "I've been trying *not* to think about it. We both know we can't get involved. First of all, you're leaving very soon. And then there's me—" He stopped talking and looked down.

"There's you what?" she asked, tilting her head.

He let out the breath he'd been holding. "Let's say you were here under very different circumstances. That your life was in Bear Ridge. I don't think I have anything left over to give after the triplets and the ranch and my family. For several reasons, really."

She stared at him, her expression unreadable. But he felt her unspoken *oh*.

"I guess that kiss got me thinking," she said. "I mean, it wasn't planned. It was spur-of-the-moment. You felt it. I felt it. So we kissed. Sometimes, you just have to go with what you *feel*, right?"

No. Sometimes you had to put aside how you felt for the greater good. Like someone's goals and aspirations. Which were not here in Bear Ridge, Wyoming. Sometimes you had to let someone go.

"I'll tell you how I feel, Wendy. I want to see you soar. I want to see you reach for the moon and stars—and grab them. I want to see all your dreams come true. That means leaving Bear Ridge and going where opportunities take you. Nothing would make me happier than to see your byline in a *New York Times* article. *Nothing*."

Something *would* rival that, actually. Like just one amazing night with Wendy in his bed. But he wouldn't say that.

She looked at him, then away. She seemed about to say something, but then a cry came from upstairs.

Wendy practically jumped. "I'll go see what's what," she said, her voice strained. And then she dashed up the stairs before he could say another word.

Follow her, he thought. *Make sure she's okay.*

No, stay right where you are.

He'd said what needed to be said. That he had nothing to give a relationship. And that he wanted—needed—her to leave town. He hadn't said that in so many words, but he'd made it clear.

He was right to stay on the sofa. And to make sure that, in the end, he would let her go. That was in *her* best interest. And when it came to him and Wendy, that was what he cared about most.

As Wendy plucked a fussy Dallas from his crib, her thoughts echoed in her head.

What if what I want has changed though?

But she couldn't say that. Not to Nash. Certainly not yet when she wasn't sure of anything except for the fact that she was falling for him. She wanted to see her byline in *The New York Times* too. But she also really liked the idea of waking up next to Nash Dawson every day and going down the hall to tend to a crying triplet.

"Everything's okay," she whispered to the sweet baby, his face a little scrunched up from dismay that he'd woken a little early from his nap. She cradled him and the way he melted against her, his head resting on her chest, made her heart swell.

Soar—to use Nash's word.

"You and your brothers are so precious," she whispered into his soft hair, walking him around the nursery in case he'd fall back asleep.

She stopped by the window and looked out, at the beautiful landscape of the ranch, the mountains in the distance. A sense of forever.

"How am I supposed to just go away when the article is done?" she whispered to Dallas. "Huh? Any idea? No? Me either. I'm just supposed to write that story and then drive back to Cheyenne, happy as can be that it's my ticket to some big exciting city and some big exciting newspaper? I'd get two seconds down the road before my feelings for your handsome uncle would turn me right around. And then there's you three. I like you and your brothers," she whispered. "A lot. A lot—a lot."

An unexpected monkey wrench.

She sucked in a breath as an idea came to her. Hmm...

She mulled it over, paced around the nursery with the little guy against her chest, gently rubbing his back, softly singing a lullaby. She looked down at the baby in her arms, at sweet Dallas Dawson, and that swell, the soar in her heart could not be ignored.

Maybe it was like what Nash had been talking about earlier. That he was so moved by the babies when he first met them but then relieved and grateful he got to go home, back to his regular life, and leave them behind. Maybe after she wrote the article, she'd get those two seconds down the road and be glad to leave them all behind, this domestic life, when she had the bright lights of big cities in her sights.

Yes, maybe it was easy to get all swoony about baby triplets when you had serious feelings for their gorgeous, thoughtful uncle. That sounded pretty reasonable.

Or maybe what she felt for the four Dawsons was just unexpectedly humongous. Maybe all that *feeling* was overtaking her heart. Overtaking *her*.

The idea kicking around in her head had some merit.

The right move at the right time.

Just like that kiss was, really. Last night, it had told her how she truly felt about Nash. That she wanted more from him. That the idea of walking away from him when she was done with the article felt unthinkable.

She'd give herself a test of sorts.

With Dallas barely awake in her arms, she headed back downstairs. Nash stood as she came into the living room.

"How would you like three uninterrupted hours to yourself?" she asked him. "To take a nap yourself. Ride out on the range and get some chores done. Work in the office. Talk to the horses. Check on your parents, uninterrupted."

While *she* babysat the triplets—all three, by herself. As a reporter, to see what it was like. And as a woman—also to see what it was like. The former could walk away after the test. The latter was in it for different reasons.

She wasn't even entirely sure what she meant. To see if she was kidding herself about even considering a life with Nash Dawson? This life. On a ranch, the very type of environment she'd longed to escape from growing up because her heart was elsewhere. With triplet babies, who'd be very demanding of her time. Who'd take over her *life*—forget about her heart.

To get his work done, Nash had to have systems and backups. If Wendy could see herself settling down with the man she loved, she'd be taking on this life. These triplets. This ranch. But she'd also want to work as a reporter, continue to pursue the work that excited her and challenged her. If Nash managed to do both, to balance work and family, why couldn't she? There was a newspaper, a good one, albeit a free weekly, right here in town. The very paper that had given teenaged Wendy in high school her first job and taught her the basics of who, what, where, when and why. Instilled solid values of how to conduct herself as a journalist. There was also a very respected daily county paper headquartered in Brewer, a half hour away. There were *options*.

You're getting way ahead of yourself, she thought, gently rubbing the baby's back. Nash just told you he didn't have anything to give a relationship. This might all be moot.

She bit her lip. But at least she'd have a better understanding of how she felt. What she wanted.

And if Nash had real feelings for her as well, that would become clear. Room in his heart, in his life, would happen naturally. Because that was how love worked, right?

He doesn't want you to stay though, a little voice inside reminded her. Then repeated it louder. *He wants you to go live your dream so that he can support you the way he didn't support his brother. Saying goodbye to you will actually help him heal.*

She bit her lip, suddenly unsure of herself. Or him. Of them.

Right now, focus on what you want, she told herself. *Where your heart is. Find out.*

"I'm listening," he said, his head tilted.

Okay. Here goes. "I want to see for myself what it's like to take care of three babies who are *not* napping," she said. "As a reporter working on a story about the four of you *and* as a woman with much more than just a crush on you, Nash Dawson."

He stared at her for a moment, his gaze going to Dallas in her arms, then back to her face. "A few hours babysitting is nothing like real life. You can't really determine anything from three hours of reading stories and feeding them and entertaining them."

Well, that went without saying.

But she realized he *was* saying this because he absolutely did not want her to stay. She swallowed, a little worried that she would love caring for the triplets on her own and that it wouldn't matter to Nash, that he was so focused on her achieving her career aspirations that he couldn't see she could want something else too.

Like everything in this room. The love, the family.

That what she wanted for herself had changed. Evolved. Grown.

"I'll be honest, Wendy," he said. "At dinner tonight, I hope the triplets make Braydon want to have children. But when it comes to you, I hope they make you want to get on a plane to New York as soon as possible."

She winced, half touched that he cared so much about her dream *and* half about to cry that he was so stubborn when it came to her feelings for him and the triplets. But she wasn't even sure his insistence that she achieve her big goals for herself, that nothing stand in her way, *was* about her.

Huh. Maybe that was what had been bothering her since their conversation in the living room over their BLTs. That this was about Nash and his broken heart, his guilt, his sorrow. And not really about her and what she wanted and needed at all. She'd need some reassurance from him.

But the whole thing was emotionally complicated. She wasn't sure of anything.

Including whether she actually could take care of three babies for three hours. Maybe she'd discover that the domestic life wasn't where her heart was. That she did just have a very big crush on a handsome rancher who'd taken in his orphaned baby nephews. The entire state of Wyoming was swooning over Nash Dawson; it was why every media outlet wanted the story. It was why she was *here*.

He looked at her for a long moment, and she saw his expression soften along with his shoulders. "Fine, babysit away. As long as you promise that if anything comes up, you'll call me immediately. *One* baby can be too much. Two can push a person over the edge. Three... If they're all crying at once. If you don't get bottles made up fast enough. If one suddenly feels gassy while another accidentally bops himself on the nose and starts screaming."

Excitement—and butterflies—overtook her and she felt like clapping. "If I feel that I need help, I'll text or call right away."

A cry came from upstairs as if on cue.

"You've got this?" he asked. "Three diapers need changing. Then bottles to make and three waiting mouths. Then their solids. Then playtime, story time, talking to them. Maybe a walk around the ranch since it's such a nice day."

"I've got this," she assured him.
But did she?
She was about to find out.

Chapter Nine

"Trying to scare me off?" Wendy asked all three Dawson babies as they sat in their high chairs awaiting their jarred food, each having a *moment*. Ryder was making a loud screechy sound that didn't seem correlated with any particular mood. Dallas was fussing—not crying but not looking very happy. Callum was banging both hands on the tray.

Wendy had been on her own with the triplets for almost an hour—and so far, so good. Well, until now. Still, this was hardly anything to call Nash about. They were all fussing because they probably wanted their oatmeal puree now and she was being a little slow.

"Hey, I'm learning here, tiny humans," she said.

After Nash had left the nursery, Wendy had felt both exhilarated and terrified. Getting the babies out of the cribs and changed into fresh diapers and back into their pj's was a lot less scary those times when Nash was there. She'd followed all the previous steps she'd watched and learned from in the past few days. Such as making good use of the playpen, careful not to take a hand or her eyes off the baby on the changing table. She'd gotten through the diaper changes pretty easily—

meaning no fussing, though she had gotten bopped on the nose by Ryder when she'd leaned over for a kiss on his forehead—so she'd been a little too confident about what came next. Getting the triplets downstairs.

With Callum and Ryder in the playpen in the nursery and Dallas the last to be changed, she'd decided to carry him into the kitchen first, get him settled in the playpen there, then hurry back up for the next baby. But the moment she'd left the nursery, Ryder started screeching. She'd attempted to soothe him but he lifted his arms, clearly wanting out and to be picked up. She'd promised him she'd be back in a jiff, then hurried out, only having to considerably slow her pace to take care going down the stairs with Dallas in her arms.

She got him in the playpen in the kitchen, ran back upstairs and plucked out Ryder, who mercifully stopped crying once she had him cradled against her and made soothing sounds. She assured Callum she'd be back in two seconds, got Ryder beside Dallas in the kitchen playpen and hurried back upstairs for the final triplet.

Her ponytail had swung in front of her shoulder, a strand of hair loosening, and Callum got his tight little fist on it, giving a yank that almost had her seeing stars. She'd gotten him downstairs and beside his brothers, then took a deep breath and tucked her hair back in the ponytail, only for Callum to start fussing. Then Ryder again.

The *noise*.

A lullaby player was attached to the side of the playpen, so she'd put on some soft tunes, then grabbed a few toys from the basket on the table and gave one to each baby. Callum had ignored the proffered squishy lion, so she set it beside him. Ryder happily took the small cloth book with chewy tabs on the edges and started gnawing away. Dallas had taken the soft rattle and immediately bopped Callum on the arm with it, and Callum startled as if in shock, then let out a huge laugh.

Oh, the relief. Wendy had been so grateful and had quickly made up the bottles, consulting the measurements hanging on the fridge by a magnet even though she'd memorized the proportions days ago. She'd wanted to get everything just right. Since the triplets were all reasonably calm and quiet, she figured she'd feed them in the kitchen instead of moving the playpen into the living room.

She'd taken Ryder out first, settled him on her lap with him slightly reclined, his head in the crook of her arm, and he happily took his bottle. She'd relaxed at how smoothly feeding number one had gone. She gave him a burp, forgetting the burp cloth entirely, and he spit up just below her shoulder, but hey, that was what she was dressed for in her T-shirt and jeans. With Ryder back in the playpen, batting the squishy lion around, she gave Callum a bottle, remembering the burp cloth this time. Same for Dallas.

She was so busy with her task at hand and on making sure the two she wasn't feeding at the moment were alive and well in the playpen that she forgot to think about how she was *feeling*—if she'd been enjoying the process. Or if it all seemed very, very hard. If she'd hand over responsibility to Nash, exhausted and relieved that this wasn't her daily life, and run for the hills.

She supposed she'd be able to assess all that later. Forty-five minutes at that point felt like barely a blip in the three hours she'd be solo with them.

With all three back in the playpen, she told them a few stories, then chattered to them while she got out the three jars of baby food and three spoons. Then she scooped each baby out and into a high chair at the table, the jars open and ready for their waiting mouths.

She remembered the bibs at the last moment, a good thing since changing all three after breakfast wasn't high on her list of things to add. That was when the fussbudgeting began.

"Okay, I'm ready, guys!" she said, making exaggerated funny faces at them as she sat down in the swivel chair at the table. "Open up!"

Dallas complied as the spoon of oatmeal and peach puree came toward his mouth. Ryder frowned and would not open up. She swiveled over to Callum with the spoonful, which got a shriek out of Ryder. She moved back to Ryder and fed him, Callum screeching now.

My goodness that was earsplitting.

Once each baby had had their first spoonful, they seemed to calm down, ready for another. She moved easily from high chair to high chair, the trio loving their lunch and making her feel like she was pretty good at this—until they didn't.

Ryder started shrieking for reasons unknown. Callum kept banging away on the tray and giggling every now and then. And as Wendy brought the final spoonful to Dallas's waiting mouth, he moved and batted it, the glob of oatmeal and peaches landing on Wendy's cheek and slightly in her ear. *Nice and cold and slimy*, she thought with a grimace. She glanced down and saw it had also got on the ends of her hair.

Figures it would be *her* who'd need to change clothes. And take a shower to get the baby cereal out of her hair completely. At least it smelled pleasantly of peaches. She grabbed a baby wipe and got rid of the cereal. *That will have to be my shower for now*, she thought with a smile.

Hmm, how to get their attention all at once. She clapped her hands excitedly, making exaggerated sounds. "Hi, boys!" she said. *Clap, clap, clap.* "What should we do now? How about some time outside? We can explore the ranch and see the herds and pastures!"

The clapping seemed to do the trick. Ryder stopped shrieking and was staring at her. Callum wasn't banging any more. Dallas was babbling. She quickly got the jars and spoons in the sink and wiped up the high chairs.

"Okay, gang, into the stroller we go!" she said with a few more claps, then plucked each baby from the high chairs. She'd noticed that Nash had brought the mammoth stroller in by the side door, where a ramp would easily lead them all down to the ground. He didn't miss a beat. That was Nash Dawson.

It was a beautiful day—sixty-eight degrees at the moment with abundant sunshine, so no fleece jackets required. She brought each baby over to the stroller and got him settled, double-checked each harness had clicked into place, then grabbed three tiny sun hats from the row of hooks near the coatrack and plopped one on each of their heads.

Nash had told her that everything she'd need would be in the stroller basket below the seats—several diapers and a pack of wipes, a few baby blankets, toys and pacifiers. She glanced there, and satisfied she'd have the basics, she opened the door and got the stroller out, then maneuvered herself behind it to shut the door. She slowly wheeled down the ramp.

"I did it, guys!" she told them. "Let's go explore our world!"

She paused, wondering if she should have changed their diapers after they ate, but she had just changed them when they'd awakened. In any case, she had fresh diapers in case their current ones got very soggy on their little excursion.

She glanced around for Nash but didn't see him anywhere. A tall ranch hand was dragging a hose near the barn so she decided to explore the opposite direction, along the path that would eventually lead toward the road. Way before that, running adjacent, was a creek bank she could walk along. The path wasn't paved so pushing the stroller might require a Herculean effort, but she'd try it out. Back when she and Nash were young friends, they'd spent a lot of time at the creek, and there were many large flat rocks to sit on if she needed a rest.

Wendy pushed the stroller toward the path, the beautiful weather and gorgeous property and three content, curious babies putting a happy skip in her step. She kept up a steady stream of chatter, pointing at the creek when it appeared after a bend around the trees and heavy brush. She looked up at the bright blue sky and few fluffy clouds, a feeling of peace settling over her. There was nowhere else she'd rather be at this moment. Not even in the exciting newsroom at the *Cheyenne Daily Gazette*.

Yeah, but it's a gorgeous spring day and the Dawson kiddos are all happy right now. No one's shrieking. No one's got a fistful of your hair. No one is spitting up on your shoulder.

Still. A newsroom, particularly at the *Gazette* but even at the *Bear Ridge Free Weekly* when she was just a high school cub reporter assisting others, had always exhilarated her. But right here, right now, she felt... happy, she realized. *Full.*

She walked on, pointing out the trees and birds and the brush and stones that sometimes jutted up in the creek. It was so peaceful out here. A good twenty minutes had passed of seeing nothing but nature and the beautiful faces of the Dawson triplets. She did love Cheyenne and living right in the bustling area of downtown even if all she could afford was that small studio apartment above a law office. But she'd spent so much energy on running from Watson Dairy and farm life that she'd forgotten how absolutely breathtaking nature was, the freshness of the air, the rugged landscape, the mountains in the distance.

"Waaah!"

Well, she had gotten pretty far without a shriek until

now. Wendy stopped and eyed the crier. Callum this time. From his scrunched up face, his red cheeks and angry blue eyes, he wasn't just being a fussbudget.

"Awww, what's wrong, sweet pea?" she cooed, unbuckling the harness and taking him out. He immediately calmed down as she held him vertically against her, gently rubbing his back, and she had the sense he needed the change in body position. "Lemme see, a little gassy, maybe?" she asked. She looked at Callum, who still seemed a bit miserable but wasn't crying. She glanced at the other two triplets. "What do you guys think?"

Dallas eyed her briefly and Ryder was babbling again. She rocked Callum, continuing to rub his back and paced in a small circle. She could smell that wonderful baby wash scent in his hair and she gave him a snuggle, her heart pinging in her chest. She looked at him, at his brothers.

"You three are so precious," she said. "So, so precious. Just look at you."

She gazed at them, dumbstruck for a moment by their curious little faces, Ryder still babbling. Dallas staring at a bird perched on a low branch. And Callum's soft, sturdy weight in her arms. *I feel so rooted*, she thought.

For the first time.

She gasped, feeling her eyes widen. Rooted. That was exactly how she felt. How strange. She wondered if it was mostly about nostalgia though. Surely it was. Having spent so much time here, along this very path, as a child. She'd always felt comfortable here. Safe. Understood. Her bestie at her side.

She'd never quite felt that same way at any of her reporter jobs, even at the *Gazette*, because she was always unsure of herself, if she'd make it. If she had what it took, if anyone would *see* her.

Nash sees you. He saw you last week when he ran into your mother. He sees you now.

She gasped again as an understanding filled her.

Nash had believed in her these past fifteen years when they hadn't said a word to each other, when they'd stopped knowing each other.

"Your Uncle Nash is something else," she whispered as her eyes felt misty with emotion, with the realization that Nash had cared about her all this time, even if somewhere deep in his heart. He'd always loved her, despite. She knew that now.

And her own heart grew ten sizes.

She shifted Callum again and reached a hand to her chest as though she could feel her heart growing.

Oh, Nash, she thought, his gorgeous face, his tall sexy body in those jeans and Western shirts overtaking her.

She snuggled the baby, and he let out a little giggle. Wendy laughed but quickly felt so overcome with emotion that she had to gulp in a breath.

"I wish I knew how to hold all three of you at once," she said. "I wonder if Nash does. Probably. The man can do anything." She'd ask him later. And if it *was* possible to somehow hold all three while standing, she wanted him to show her. So she could snuggle the triplets all at once, so they'd feel how much she adored them.

Ryder let out a "ba la" and Callum rested his hand on Wendy's neck. Dallas was waving his hands at two birds that suddenly flew off a branch.

I don't have to wonder where my heart is, she thought. *It's right here. Right now. With these three.*

And with Nash Dawson, somewhere on the range. She wondered what Nash was doing at this exact moment. Where he was. What he was thinking.

She missed him. She wished he was here right now as she was experiencing all these new feelings, these new thoughts.

"Did you guys know that your Uncle Nash and I used to come here all the time when we were kids?" she said to the triplets. "Right there," she added, shifting Callum to her hip and using her free hand to quickly point at a spot between trees. "We used to sit on that huge flat rock and just stare out at the water and talk. About everything."

She smiled at the memories that came fast and furious. Nash telling her that one day he'd run the Dawson Brothers Cattle Ranch and that he liked knowing that his life was mapped out like that. Wendy could remember thinking that she wanted the opposite—having no idea where her dreams would take her as long as she was an investigative journalist, telling important stories. Nash had once asked what she'd meant by that—important— and she'd had to think about it. She'd explained she was talking about writing articles that people cared about, that made people *understand*—sometimes a different point of view too.

You'll definitely be writing those articles, he'd said. *I have no doubt of that. You always help me see another side. Like with Ethan when I have to pick up his slack.*

He'd complain about his brother and Wendy would try to help him understand that Ethan just didn't see the ranch the same way Nash did. She'd often compare it to how she felt about the farm and that made it easy for him not to demonize Ethan as a young teenager who wanted to spend all his spare time practicing bronc riding. But then they'd stopped talking at thirteen and he probably turned all that resentment toward his brother inward and it had festered as they years passed.

To the point that his heart is closed, she realized. He'd told her, flat out, that he had nothing left to give after taking care of the boys and the ranch and seeing to his parents and grandmother. Nothing left for a relationship—with her.

She felt a prick to her heart and winced. She'd learned long ago the importance of listening—believing someone—when they made it clear how they felt about you. About her. Nash had left no doubt fifteen years ago that he hadn't returned her feelings. She'd accepted it instead of continuing to harbor hope as she had when she first realized a couple years prior that she had developed a major romantic crush on her buddy. Now, at twenty-eight, with some life experience and failed romances under her belt, was no time to start wishing he might change his mind about what he said.

But isn't that what tonight is all about? she thought

suddenly, her sister's worried face coming to mind. *Helping Braydon see things differently, shift the way he was looking at the subject of having children?*

Wendy gave Callum a little rock in her arms, a sigh escaping her.

Everything was so complicated.

"You seem to feel better, Cal," she said to the baby she held. "Let's get you back in the stroller and resume our walk, okay?"

But she found herself not wanting to let go of Callum. She loved the feel of him in her arms, that sturdy little weight, his baby-shampoo-scented hair, the way his big blue eyes latched onto her face. "How did I get attached to you and your brothers so fast?" she whispered. "What kind of magic spell did you put on me?"

"La ba," Callum said, pressing his tiny hand to her neck.

Her heart squeezed and she snuggled him again. *You are attached—no question there.*

A bunch of questions started knocking around in her head that she didn't have answers to, so she got Callum settled between his brothers and started walking again. *You're just swept up in a whirlwind of these intense days with the man you loved for so long and his sweet orphaned nephews. You're writing their story. Of course you're attached.*

It doesn't mean you suddenly want to get married and raise three babies.

It doesn't mean you suddenly want to give up your dreams of The New York Times *or* The Boston Globe.

She only knew that something had seriously shifted inside her. Not changed, exactly.

It was similar to the way she'd felt her heart expanding earlier. Things were moving around in there. And in her head.

Unsettled, she pulled her phone from her back pocket to check the time. Another hour had passed. Forty-five minutes left to her...test. A test she had no idea how to score.

She heard footsteps and another sound that she couldn't quite figure out, and suddenly a petite elderly woman with a white bob and two walking sticks came around the bend in the path.

The familiar face of Livvy Dawson, Nash's grandmother, lit up at the sight of her. "Wendy! And my great-grands! I'd give you a big hug but I've got these things," she said, lifting the walking sticks.

Wendy grinned and turned the stroller around so the triplets were facing their great-grandmother. "It's so nice to see you. I'm babysitting for a few hours."

Livvy's eyes shone with surprise. "These triplets happen to be the greatest babies in all the world. But even their great-grandnana has to admit that three at once is a lot. How's it been going?"

"They've been wonderful. I've been taking care of them since they woke from their nap, so I've gotten a real education about their routine—diaper-changing and bottle-feeding and solids and then entertaining them. I've loved every minute of it but I'm also ready for a nap myself."

Livvy laughed. "I once babysat all three for about

an hour and that was something. When my son and daughter-in-law came to relieve me, I fell into a deep sleep for hours. The triplets are adorable but *exhausting*." She smiled at her great-grandchildren, then at Wendy. "I can tell from the way you're looking at them that they've won you over with those giant cheeks."

"They definitely have. They're just such marvels. I can't get over them. Every little thing feels magical."

Livvy beamed. "Well if you're in the market for a husband and instant triplets, I know a very handsome single rancher and three babies who would love a mama."

Wendy gasped. She definitely wasn't expecting *that* from the conversation.

"If you remember, I always did speak my mind," Livvy said. "We always thought you and Nash would end up married one day. We being his parents and me."

Wendy let out a hard sigh. "I used to dream of marrying Nash back when I had a secret crush on him. But that got blown to bits. Then fifteen years go by without a single word between us, and suddenly—" She stopped and bit her lip.

"And suddenly?" Livvy prompted, her blue eyes twinkling.

And suddenly I'm falling hard for him all over again. And this time, he comes with baby triplets who I've gotten very attached to.

But Wendy knew she didn't have to say any of that. It was plain on her face, in her voice.

"Things are complicated," Wendy said. "I live in Cheyenne, for one. With big plans to move to a major city to advance in my career as a journalist. And Nash has made it crystal clear that he doesn't have anything left to give a relationship anyway. Between the triplets and the ranch, he has a full plate. So it's probably best that we just ignore any…interest."

Livvy raised an eyebrow. "Want some advice?"

Wendy could feel her face light up. "Absolutely."

"Don't," Livvy said. "Don't ignore interest. Don't ignore your feelings, for heaven's sake. You're here for a reason, Wendy Watson."

"For the *story*."

"Yes, the story. Which you're living at the moment."

Wendy swallowed. She glanced at the triplets, babbling in the stroller, all three engaged by all the interesting sights around them, from the birds to the leaves to the creek to the grown-ups talking. "The firsthand experience with caring for them will be helpful in writing a truly in-depth—"

"Oh, I'm sure," Livvy interrupted with a sly smile. "And maybe you're learning all sorts of things."

Wendy's shoulders sagged as some truths bubbled up inside her. "The past year or so I've been feeling a little antsy. At first, I thought it was that my career just wasn't going the way I'd hoped, that I just wasn't getting the promotions I'd worked so hard for or any chances to write a story that would show my bosses what I could do. But when I'd go out to work events or weddings or be invited out with couple friends, I began to understand that what I was missing seemed more personal than professional. That I felt so…alone all the time."

"And so you put more of your time and energy into your career, looking to fill yourself up there since getting that big break was always your goal. And you probably chastised yourself too for even caring about finding your Mr. Right."

Wendy stared at Nash's wise grandmother in surprise. "Yes, exactly. I've always been about self-empowerment." She shook her head. "My whole life I've wanted to be a big-city reporter. Suddenly, I'm thinking of settling down in small town—my own hometown? Being a wife and mom?" She grimaced and felt her cheeks heat up. "Not that anyone's asked," she quickly added. She was getting way ahead of herself.

Livvy smiled gently. "Who says you can't have both? Mix the two? When I first started out as a nurse, I worked in the ER in triage. I'd planned to work helivac. But then I fell in love and suddenly I wanted other things too. So I found a way to make *both* dreams work for me and I became a school nurse to suit my hours as a working mom."

Wendy felt herself brighten. "That's wonderful." There certainly were newspapers everywhere.

"One more piece of advice from an eighty-one-year-old who's seen a few things in life," Livvy added. "You don't have to know everything. Just follow your heart, whatever that means, wherever it takes you. The heart always knows."

Wendy smiled. "That's great advice. Because that's all anyone can do, right?"

Livvy nodded. "Hold these for a sec, will you?" she asked, handing over her walking sticks. "I want to give my grandbabies a kiss each on their sweet heads before I shuffle off."

Wendy took the sticks and watched the loving great-grandnana press a kiss to each triplet's soft hair.

"The heart knows," Livvy said, taking back the sticks. Then she nodded and kept going.

Wendy watched her retreating form until Livvy was around another bend, then turned to the triplets. For a moment, she was lost in thought about all the woman had said. But it was overwhelming too, so she blinked it out of her head for now. "Well, Dawson boys. I guess we'll turn around and go back to the house. Not that I'm remotely ready to end solo time with you three sweet cherubs."

She started pushing the stroller along the path, then stopped in her tracks for a moment when she realized that if she followed her heart *right now*, it would take her exactly where she was headed.

Chapter Ten

Nash was once again in the very grocery store where he'd run into Wendy's mom last week. A half hour ago, he'd texted Wendy to ask for her shopping list for tonight's dinner. She'd texted back the ingredients for linguini carbonara, most of which he had in the fridge or pantry. *And if you want to pick up some Italian bread, that would be great,* she'd added.

He checked his basket against the texted list. Italian bread, check. Linguini, which apparently was apparently Braydon Hanley's favorite pasta, check. Garlic, check. Heavy cream, check. Everything else he had. Grocery shopping sure was a breeze when he didn't have a triple stroller of babies with him.

He turned to head toward the registers, nodding or waving at people he knew. A guy he'd gone to school with was pushing a cart with a toddler sitting on the little seat behind the push bar. His wife, who'd been a year behind them, wore a baby in a sling on her torso. They were deep in conversation about how the diapers they preferred—softer with a faint baby powder scent—were never on sale but they thought those were worth the extra money. Then the guy remembered they were almost out of coffee and turned down an aisle.

Nash wistfully watched them go, the woman slinging an arm around her husband's waist as they stopped to scan the coffee selection.

Nice, he thought with an inward sigh. The partnership. Here they were, talking diapers and coffee, the most ordinary of topics of conversation, and on the ride home they might talk about their worries—that the toddler was behind on a milestone. That the baby wasn't yet over his cold. That the property taxes increased again. It would be nice to have someone to share everything with. The big, the small. The ordinary, the extraordinary.

Nash felt something pinching in his chest and absently rubbed the spot. *What is this?* he asked himself. Some kind of unsettling awareness—of something. That he wanted what that couple had.

He looked down at his phone, at the text from Wendy with the list of ingredients. He liked it, liked the everyday quality of it.

Because it makes you feel like you're not alone. Like you have a partner.

And you can talk to Wendy about anything. Whether linguini or babies or how gut-wrenching it is to think about your last conversation with your brother.

A subject that kept coming up in his mind now that the six-month mark of the loss was drawing so close. Just two days away.

He wished Wendy was beside him, slipping an arm

around *his* waist while grabbing something he might have forgotten off a shelf.

And if she decided she did want to stick around in Bear Ridge, give what was between them a real shot? If he'd let anyone close to him, it would be Wendy Watson.

But he couldn't bear the thought of her giving up on her lifelong goals—especially for him, a man with truly nothing left over to give a relationship. He hadn't been making excuses when he'd said that after the triplets, the ranch and his family, he was spent. In all ways, including his heart. He could feel how closed off he was. And Wendy, so full of life and vitality and energy, deserved much more than someone who couldn't give her his time, let alone himself.

I'll be honest, Wendy. At dinner tonight, I hope the triplets make Braydon want to have children. But when it comes to you, I hope they make you want to get on a plane to New York as soon as possible.

He'd seen her wince and had instantly regretted being so direct, so matter of fact. But then again, that was better than mixed signals. Like kissing her and then pulling away.

I guess that kiss got me thinking, he recalled her saying. *I mean, it wasn't planned. It was spur-of-the-moment. You felt it. I felt it. So we kissed. Sometimes, you just have to go with what you feel, right?*

If she wanted to go with it—and he couldn't stop thinking about kissing her again, about much more—then why was he preventing it? Did he think he knew what she wanted better than she did? Did he think he knew her own mind better than she did?

Of course he didn't.

But...doing the right thing was doing the right thing. Even when sometimes, it felt...wrong.

Great. Now he was even more mixed up.

He glanced at his phone for the time—he'd better get back to the house. Wendy's three hours of babysitting would be up in twenty minutes and it would take almost that long to get back to the ranch.

He was about to pass the flower display when he thought a bouquet for the dining table would be a nice touch for tonight. He eyed the offerings and chose one he thought Wendy would like. Pretty and colorful and abundant. Like she was.

"I guess someone has a date."

Nash turned and immediately tensed at the site of Laurel Parker, who he'd dated for a month right before he'd lost Ethan. When he'd gotten the terrible news, very little except his loss, the triplets and his family had entered his consciousness, and he'd realized he hadn't even called Laurel to tell her about the accident. He and his parents and grandmother had driven down to Cheyenne and stayed a few nights in Ethan and Lydia's house and he'd ignored his phone—the texts and calls, including from Laurel, who of course had heard since the crash had been all over the news.

The day he returned home, the triplets now living with him, she came knocking on his door with condolences, arms outstretched, and he stayed frozen in place in the doorway. He barely said anything, unable to think, to process, but aware nonetheless that Laurel had not felt like a source of comfort to him. And with the triplets crying inside, he told her he had to go, that he was their legal guardian now and he wouldn't have time or energy for a relationship. Her eyes had widened in surprise or shock. He wasn't even sure he'd said he was sorry, but he'd been a mess at the time.

He hadn't thought about that in a long time. They hadn't been all that serious or even exclusive at that point, but he'd seen her a few times a week. He'd been cold to her though, and he'd never even apologized.

Just like he'd let things go with Wendy fifteen years ago when she ran away from him.

That's how cowards act, he thought, mentally shaking his head. *You can't run from what you can't deal with.*

But that had always been his way, he knew now.

He looked directly at Laurel, whose chin was lifted, her hazel eyes assessing him. "Laurel, I owe you an apology for how I acted the night you came over after—" He paused and took a breath. "I was a wreck about my brother and I was unfair to you. I'm sorry about that."

She offered a cold smile and tossed her long dark ponytail behind her shoulder. "No worries. That night I came over I had no idea you were taking in your infant nephews. My God, Nash—if we were still a couple, I'd probably look *forty* years old right now. Didn't take me long at all to realize I dodged a bullet when you dumped me."

Jeez. Well, he certainly wouldn't worry about her feelings anymore.

She walked off, luckily not in the direction of the registers, where he was headed.

Wendy was waiting for him at home. He let himself focus on that and all thoughts of this nasty little run-in left his head.

Thinking about Wendy had a way of making everything okay.

Until he remembered that she'd just spent the past three hours on her own with the triplets. And she also might feel that his determination to see her leave Bear Ridge when she had what she needed for the article would mean she too had dodged a bullet.

That was supposed to be in *his* best interest. So he could do right by her. The way he hadn't with Ethan.

And now nothing was making any sense.

He put the bouquet of flowers back in their plastic vase. Suddenly, bringing Wendy flowers, even for the dinner table when they were having guests, felt…off.

Just like he did.

At just before 6:00 p.m. that night, Wendy stood at the stove in Nash's kitchen, stirring the bacon, onion and garlic in the sauté pan. She glanced at the big silver pot on the back burner. Another minute and the linguini would be done. Nash was at the counter, mixing together the parmesan, cream and egg yolks for the carbonara, seemingly in deep concentration on his task. Wendy had offered to prepare everything, but he'd wanted to help.

Something was clearly on his mind. When he'd gotten home earlier this afternoon, she'd told him all about her three hours with the triplets, sharing funny details about the oatmeal and peach puree on her cheek, in her ear, in her hair and more trying times that involved screeching and squawking. And how she'd loved every second of it. She'd mentioned running into his grandmother by the creek—but not a peep about their conversation—and how enchanted she'd been by the way the triplets laughed and babbled and stared at their surroundings with such alert curiosity. As she'd talked, she could feel how animated and excited she was. She still wasn't sure if it was novelty or something bigger, much deeper than that. All she knew was that she'd had a truly magical time.

Nash had listened, asking a few questions, but he'd been distracted—and that was probably understating his mood. There was a strain etched into his handsome face. The triplets were napping then, so he'd gone to say a quiet hello to them and she'd finally taken a much-needed shower. By the time she came out, clean again and refreshed, he'd said the triplets were still asleep and that he was going to get some work done in the office.

He'd disappeared and the house had been very quiet. At some point, she heard the upstairs shower running and a door opening and closing. A fussy sound was followed by Nash's voice but she couldn't quite make out what he was saying to the triplets. She was in the kitchen then, going over the recipe for the linguini carbonara, getting out the pot for the pasta and the sauté pan. Then she'd gone into the guest room for a while to give him some space, wondering, worrying just what had him so turned around. Something about his expression had told her not to pry, to let him just have some privacy with his thoughts.

About twenty minutes ago, he'd appeared in the kitchen, in jeans and a button-down Western shirt, to ask how he could help with dinner. He seemed a little more present but she could tell that something was very much on his mind. Just when she couldn't *not* ask if he was okay, and had decided to, he went upstairs to move the triplets from their nursery playpen to the one in the living room. He then made himself very busy, either setting the dining table on the deck—it was so nice out that they'd decided to eat outdoors—or cutting half of the Italian bread and pouring a few small bowls of infused olive oil to dip into.

The doorbell rang just as she slid the other half of the bread, laden with butter and garlic, into the oven. She quickly washed her hands and went with Nash to greet her sister and Braydon.

Their guests stood on the porch. Braydon—tall, blond with pale brown eyes—looked a bit nervous. Tess, her strawberry blond wavy hair in a low ponytail, appeared hopeful. Each carried something—Braydon was holding a box from her favorite bakery in town, and Tess had a beautiful bouquet of flowers.

"Thank you both," Wendy said, taking the flowers and box. "I'm so glad you guys could come."

Braydon smiled. "Pecan pie. Tess said it's your favorite."

Wendy grinned. "It absolutely is. Thank you. Tess, you know Nash from around town of course, and,

Braydon, Nash mentioned that he's a customer of your family's feedstore."

Braydon nodded and extended his hand to Nash. "I know things must be very busy at this house so it was really nice of you to invite us to dinner."

"Sure is quiet," Tess said as Nash led the way into the living room. "Are the triplets napping?"

"Ba la!" came a cheery voice as if on cue.

Tess and Braydon laughed, sharing a warm look between them—which Wendy took as a good sign. Braydon certainly didn't seem tense and closed off.

"They're chilling with their toys," Nash said as they all walked over to the playpen. Callum looked up and immediately held out his arms, but Ryder and Dallas were content to bat their stuffies on the floor of the playpen.

She was glad to see Nash more relaxed. Maybe having company and a mission was distracting him from whatever had been on his mind since he'd gotten home.

Nash scooped up Callum and turned to face everyone. The little guy was staring at Braydon and reached out a hand in the direction of the pearlized buttons on Braydon's shirt.

Braydon laughed. "You like the button?" he asked, stepping a bit closer. He smiled at Callum, who was now staring intently at him.

"He sure finds your face interesting," Wendy said with a chuckle.

She watched Braydon's expression go from sort of amused to...pained, if she wasn't mistaken. Braydon turned away and looked at the family photos lining the mantel of the huge stone fireplace. He moved closer, seeming to study each one.

"I still can't believe he's gone," Braydon said suddenly, still facing the photos. He turned then toward Nash. He shook his head. "Three babies orphaned, just like that."

The room went pin quiet.

"Every night," Nash said, moving closer to where Braydon stood, now staring again at the family photos, "when I put the triplets to bed, I tell them their mommy and daddy in Heaven love them. That their grandparents and great grandmother love them. That Uncle Nash loves them. Every night for six months now. I guess it's become tradition."

"That's beautiful," Tess said, her eyes misting with tears.

Wendy nodded, too choked up to speak for a moment. She'd never forget that first night she'd helped with bedtime and heard Nash say those words. Her eyes had gotten teary then too.

"Anything can happen," Braydon said, staring down at the floor now. "Life changes in an instant." His voice had gone a bit hollow.

A ding sounded from the kitchen. "Ah, the oven timer for the garlic bread," Wendy said. A glance at Braydon told her he was glad for the interruption—from the focus on him and the conversation. "Back in a minute."

"I'll help," Nash said to her, then turned to Tess and Braydon. "It's such a nice night that we figured we'd eat outside. Why don't you two go out and get comfortable." He gestured to the sliding glass doors that led to the deck. "Help yourself to iced tea. And you, my friend," he said to the baby in his arms, "can join your brothers."

Wendy turned as she was about to go into the kitchen. Braydon seemed strained now, much like Nash looked earlier. He didn't look at Callum as Nash set him in the playpen. Tess put a hand on his shoulder and they headed outside, closing the door behind them.

In the kitchen, Nash got the garlic bread out of the oven and cut it up, putting it in a napkin-lined basket along with the plain Italian bread, while Wendy poured the bacon, onion and garlic into the pot of linguini, then stirred in the sauce.

"Do you think Braydon's feelings about having kids have anything to do with Ethan and the triplets?" Nash whispered as Wendy used two serving spoons to mix the pasta.

Wendy paused and stared at him. She hadn't connected the two until now. But suddenly everything made sense. "Tess said he got quieter, more subdued a few months ago," she whispered back. "And that he wouldn't open up about why. She knew he was a big fan of Ethan's, but because he didn't talk about it, she figured it was more about the feedstore going through some financial difficulties and a close friend was having some marital troubles. But the shop and his friend's marriage bounced back these past couple of months."

Nash seemed to take that all in. "What Braydon said—'three babies orphaned, just like that' and 'how life changes an instant.' Sounds like he was deeply affected by Ethan's loss and what it meant for his newborns. Maybe once the shock of that lifted, he started thinking about the babies left behind."

Wendy pressed a hand to her heart as an ache formed there. "The fragility of life," she said, her voice low. "It must have really scared him."

Nash was quiet for a moment. "It scares me too."

She wanted to pull him into a hug, just wrap her arms around him and comfort him, let him know she understood. But he was picking up the big bowl of pasta. As if he'd known she was about to fling herself into his arms.

"I'll bring this out," he said. "Then I'll move the playpen to the deck."

Her heart heavy, Wendy followed with the bread basket. She noticed Braydon staring into the playpen as Nash brought it outside and settled it between the table and doors.

"Think they'll be rodeo champs someday?" Braydon asked as Wendy and Nash sat down. Now his gaze was on the three babies.

Nash smiled. "I'm a big believer in people going after their dreams. If the rodeo is what lights them up, I'll be their biggest supporter. And if one wants to be an accountant, another a cowboy and the third a circus performer—all good with me."

Tess smiled. "I love that."

Wendy did too. And she knew he meant it.

"That's really great," Braydon said with a nod but he still seemed subdued.

"In fact it's why Wendy is even here in town," Tess

said to her boyfriend. "I told you a little about that. How every news outlet in the state wanted an interview with Nash about how he took in his baby nephews and that he said no for the past six months. Until *Wendy's* newspaper called and he saw an opportunity to help her achieve her dreams by getting that big story."

Braydon pushed his linguini around on his plate. "I'd pay three times the cost of the paper to read that article."

Nash smiled. "It helps to know that, actually. I was so focused on what the media would gain from my agreeing to an interview that I forgot to focus on what Ethan's *fans* would gain. You said life can change in an instant, and it sure did when that decision of mine brought Wendy back into my life."

Wendy noticed her sister's ears perk up at that statement.

"What a nice thing to say," Tess said with a soft smile.

That seemed to change the tension in the air, and they ate, the guests complimenting the food, and they talked about the changes in town since Wendy had moved to Cheyenne.

"Waah!"

Ryder.

Braydon almost jumped at the sudden cry, his eyes focused on the crier.

Nash popped up and picked up his little nephew, clad in his trademark blue. He sat back down with the baby cradled in his arms. Ryder immediately grabbed his nose.

"That's some grip," Nash said with a laugh.

"He's okay now?" Braydon asked, watching intently.

"Sure," Nash said. "Sometimes they cry because they want to be picked up. To stretch out their bodies. Or because their tummies are bothering them. Or because the wind blew." He smiled. "You just never know. But if a fussbudget baby quiets down right away, then you know he just wanted this." He gave Ryder a snuggle, the baby letting go of his nose.

Braydon stared at Ryder, and Wendy wished she could read his mind. Was all this settling something for him? Changing how he felt? Or was he so affected by seeing the triplets in the flesh that he'd be even more adamant about not having kids? That it was too scary, that anything could happen in an instant.

The fragility of life.

Nash played a round of peekaboo with Ryder, who let out his huge baby laugh, and Braydon's entire face changed—with delight this time.

But then his smile faded. Wendy could see her sister notice and the strain back in her own expression.

"You're so good with the triplets, Nash," Tess said.

Nash smiled. "I wasn't always, trust me. Those early weeks, I was a walking wreck. How I got through those days I'll never know. But when you need to take care of something—something precious—you just do it. This little guy and his brothers got me through. So I guess I do know how I did it."

Braydon seemed to be listening intently.

Nash settled Ryder back in the playpen, and they resumed eating. Soon enough, plates were empty and the bread basket contained nothing but crumbs. Nash insisted on clearing the table since Wendy had cooked, which from the look on Tess's face had earned Nash even more points.

Tess walked over to the playpen and played peekaboo with the triplets, the baby laughter making them all laugh.

Dallas put his arms up, his big blue eyes focused on Tess's face.

"Awww," Tess said. "All right if I pick him up?"

"Go ahead," Wendy said—then realized she was speaking for Nash, who'd taken a stack of plates into the kitchen. Her cheeks flushed a bit.

Wendy watched her sister's face melt as she snuggled the baby against her.

"Aww," Tess murmured again. "He's so light. And smells delicious." She was gazing at the baby with such sweet wistfulness.

Wendy glanced at Braydon, whose expression was now actually pained. Uh-oh. Maybe this wasn't the best idea, after all. Had this dinner made things worse? Better? Wendy had no idea.

She figured she'd give the couple a bit of time alone and grabbed the glasses and brought them into the kitchen.

"I have no idea how to read what's going on," Wendy said to Nash, who was loading the dishwasher. "If this helped or hurt."

Nash looked at her and seemed to be thinking about exactly that. "I have an idea," he said.

"Whatever it is, I'm for it." She trusted him, plain and simple.

"It involves you and Tess watching the triplets for fifteen, twenty minutes. That okay?"

"Definitely." Though her sister was clearly wistful in the presence of the babies, feeling that way might help *Tess* understand how she felt. If she knew in her heart of hearts that she could not imagine life without motherhood in her future...

She and Nash headed back outside.

"Braydon," Nash said as they stepped onto the deck, "if you don't mind, I could use your opinion on how much supplemental feed I should order for next month. Take a walk with me out to the barn to check my inventory?"

"Sure," Braydon said, bolting up and brightening. Escaping babyland and his girlfriend holding a triplet against her chest and looking like there was nothing she wanted more seemed like a lifeline to him.

Whatever Nash was planning, she hoped it had good results. She walked over to where Tess stood in front of the playpen, still gazing at Ryder, the look in her sister's eyes unmistakable. She wanted to be a mother.

Me too, Wendy thought and then froze.

The truth about that was as undeniable as her feelings for Nash Dawson.

Chapter Eleven

To help Braydon feel more comfortable, Nash kept the conversation on the feed supply and the herd as they walked down to the barn. He could see the guy relaxing beside him. Nash knew how that worked; whenever he was overwhelmed, he'd involve himself in the ranch, whether manual labor or paperwork, and the familiarity, his comfort level, would have him feeling better in no time.

He figured that if Braydon did want to open up, whether a little or a lot, Nash would give him that opportunity by getting outside, away from other ears, away from the triplets. He wouldn't pry or prompt. He'd just let Braydon talk if he wanted to.

"The triplets are really cute," Braydon said as they headed into the barn. Nash led the way to the feed locker, where he had big bags of the supplemental feed.

Nash glanced at Braydon. That statement was a good sign that he did want to talk. "They look so much like Ethan," Nash said, which was not only true but a good opening if the guy wanted to take it.

"I used to want kids," Braydon said, his voice shaky. He looked down at the ground. "But ever since I heard about the plane crash and thought about those three infants—suddenly orphaned. Their parents and one entire set of grandparents. Gone. Just like that." He shook his head. "My mother died when I was three." He looked up at Nash for a moment, then away. "Do you know that I can't even remember her? If I didn't have pictures, I'd have no idea what she looked like."

"I'm very sorry," Nash said. "That's rough. At any age, but to lose your mom so young."

"The past few months I've been thinking a lot about the triplets. How their parents are gone. I know they're in good hands with you. I know they have their paternal grandparents. But I just keep thinking—how can I do that to my own kids?"

Nash tilted his head. "What do you mean, Braydon? Do what?"

"Put them through that. That pain. That lifelong heartbreak that'll be with them every damned day of their life. Why have kids at all when a drunk driver can take me out any day of the week. Or I get cancer. Or I slip and crack my head so hard I'm gone in a flash."

Nash swallowed, his heart clenching for Braydon.

"I mean, you're done, right?" Braydon asked. "You'd never have a kid of your own for the same reasons."

Nash hadn't given that a single thought since he'd taken in the triplets. But now that the question was raised, he thought about it hard. "Well, actually, I would."

Braydon stared at him in disbelief. "Really? Even though they could lose everything at any time?" He was looking at Nash like he had four heads.

"I mean, three children are enough, certainly. Especially all at once. But after raising these guys for the past six months—there's nothing more life-affirming, nothing more magical than taking care of them. It's probably the only thing that I know for sure." As he'd said the words, he realized how true they were, how much he'd meant them. "Those babies keep me going. Every day, I have purpose. They remind me that the world is bigger than what's going on with me—in my head."

Braydon seemed to be taking all that in, but from his expression, Nash could tell that it just didn't make sense to the guy.

"I don't know," Braydon said. "Seems safer all around to just—" He stopped talking and took a breath, looking away.

"Just drop out?" Nash finished for him, pretty sure that had been what Braydon had meant. "I guess I also try to think about what my brother and Lydia would have wanted for their boys. And I know what that is."

Braydon was staring at him, listening hard, Nash could see. "And what's that?"

"To give raising the triplets everything I have. All of me. Everything I am. That means putting them first. So that's how I operate." He sucked in a breath as he recalled a conversation he'd had with his parents a couple of days after the accident. They'd made a vow that the three of them would never travel together by plane or even by car if they could easily help it. So that if God forbid there was a loss, the triplets wouldn't be... He had a feeling that Ethan and Lydia just hadn't considered it when they'd all boarded that plane—perhaps used to everything being okay, everything working out. "I know that's all Ethan would want. You might look at things that way," he added gently. "What you think your mom might want for you. How she'd hope you'd live your life. Even though you didn't have a chance to know her. You've heard stories about her your whole life, right?"

Braydon seemed to brighten for a moment but he also seemed unsure. Listening, taking it in, but Nash had no idea if anything he was saying would chip at the wall Braydon had erected around himself.

"I think about what Tess wants," Braydon said. "I think about it all the time. She wants a houseful of kids. And that's why I think we should just end things. So she can find the right guy. Someone who wants five kids like she does. *One* kid, even. I want Tess to have everything she dreams of. So that's why I should walk away."

Oh, damn. If that was where this conversation had taken Braydon, Nash had blown it.

Braydon looked so miserable at what he'd just said that it was possible he wouldn't be able to just walk away. That maybe there was room here for more thought, some work on this very big, emotional issue. Talking it over helped. But Braydon would need to come to some important truths on his own.

"You're good on feed for at least two months," Braydon said suddenly, looking in the open feed locker. It was clear he didn't want to talk more on the subject of babies and the future. "The pastures are in such great condition that you're solid."

"Good to know, thanks."

"You and Wendy a couple?" Braydon asked as they turned to head out.

"No. I mean, we probably would be, but my life is here and hers is in Cheyenne and then a big city somewhere at a major newspaper. That's her dream. And I'd never let anything stand in the way of her achieving her goals."

Braydon nodded. "I feel the same way about Tess."

Nash froze. Wait a minute. Yes, Braydon had just said that a minute ago. But... He wanted to tell Braydon that it wasn't the same thing. But as he thought about, he supposed it was. Except in this case, making sure Tess's dream of motherhood could come true would mean she'd get her heart broken by the guy she wanted to marry.

And making sure Wendy's dream came true meant working overtime to stop thinking about a future with her. He had to let her go. He had to.

But when it came to Braydon—What? He wracked his brain for an easy difference. But there wasn't one.

How the hell had this gotten so confusing?

Two hours later, Tess and Braydon had long said goodbye, the kitchen was sparkling clean, the triplets were asleep for the night—quite possibly—and Wendy sat with Nash on the sofa, two mugs of decaf and two slices of the pecan pie that their guests had brought.

They hadn't had dessert earlier. When Nash and Braydon had returned in about twenty minutes, Tess had taken one look at her distracted, subdued boyfriend and said they should get going, and Braydon had immediately perked up as if he'd had about all he could take of babies and serious conversation. Not that Wendy had known then what Nash and Bradyon had talked about but she did now.

"My heart hurts for both of them," she said, then wrapped her hands around her mug of coffee. "I think your advice to him was so thoughtful—to ask himself what his mother would want for him. Telling him how you asked yourself what Ethan would want for his triplets and trying to focus on that most of all."

Nash had cut a piece of pie with his fork but just stared at it. "I'm not sure I did any good though. He's really torn up about how he feels. And I think I made it worse."

"How?" she asked, butterflies letting loose in her stomach.

"He asked if we were a couple, and I told him we couldn't be because my life is here and yours is in Cheyenne, and that there was no way I'd be responsible for standing in the way of your dreams."

She tilted her head. "How did that make things worse?" It made things worse for them because he was really stuck on this when *she* wasn't.

"He immediately related it to Tess's dream to be a mom. And that the best way to make her dreams come true was to end their relationship. So that he wouldn't be the one standing in *her* way."

"Oh, no," she said, her heart sinking. "It's so clear he loves Tess."

What wasn't clear was how Nash felt about *her*. Maybe it was easy for him to keep focusing on her goals and aspirations because he *wasn't* falling for her.

"What do you think will happen with Tess and Braydon?" he asked, sipping his coffee. "Will he come around?"

"I wish I knew. If only I had a crystal ball—one that actually worked," she added with as much of a smile as she could muster. "I do have a theory, if you want to hear it."

"Of course I do."

She put down her mug and leaned forward a bit. "I think that sometimes, people can get scared, worried, nervous, and so they focus on one part of the whole and use it as a lifeboat to cling to."

He seemed to be thinking about that. He took another drink of his coffee. "Like that maybe Braydon is more scared about the idea of committing to forever, so he's focusing on the scariest part about having kids. It gives him something concrete as a reason."

"Exactly," she said, nodding. "I don't want to dismiss how his mother's loss and the death of one of his idols made him feel. I know that's very real. But that's about fear—not about whether or not he wants to be a parent. Am I making any sense?"

Nash nodded. "I get the sense he does want to be a dad someday, just like he always he said he did. But yeah—the fear of something happening, his own child going through what he went through. Three infants left fatherless out of the blue. It has him in a grip."

Like you with trying to make some peace with your-

self about not supporting Ethan in his dreams. Like you not letting us even explore this beautiful thing between us...

Say it, she told herself. *Tell him how you feel. Tell him being here, on this ranch, with him and the triplets, has also become a dream.*

I can't. Because I'm scared too, she realized, her heart thudding in her chest. *Scared of getting rejected all over again.*

He picked up his mug and sat up straighter, leaning back a bit, as if putting a little physical—and emotional—distance between them. "I meant to ask you this afternoon. Do you think you have what you need for the article? If you have any questions, I could answer them now."

And then you can leave, she mentally finished for him.

A lump formed in her throat. She'd leave and go back to Cheyenne. Write the story, send it to him for approval, then turn it into her boss and see where this big front-page story took her...

But she wanted to stay right here. And she knew it. She couldn't imagine leaving. Nash. The triplets. She *couldn't*.

"I, uh, have most of what I need," she said, trying to stall for time. "But I do have a few more questions."

"Shoot," he said. He looked so much more relaxed now that they were back on this subject.

"You said that you have nothing to give a romantic relationship," she said. "That after caring for the triplets, running the ranch and watching over your family, you're just spent. I completely understand that. But what if the right woman came along when you were least expecting it. Someone who'd be very happy settling down on this ranch with you and the triplets."

He stared at her, putting the mug down again. "Wendy, I think we should just be very honest with each other right now. Is this a general question for the article or...are you talking about yourself?"

She felt her cheeks burn. "I might be talking about myself." So much for being very honest. She was feeling way too vulnerable to just say, *Yes, dammit, of course I am.*

"And what about New York? LA? *The Boston Globe*?" he asked.

"What about you and Dallas and Ryder and Callum? Why are my personal feelings for the four Dawsons any less important than my professional goals? Why does it have to be a choice?"

"Because Bear Ridge, Wyoming, isn't New York City," he said, concern in his eyes. "Here we've got the *Bear Ridge Free Weekly*. That's it."

"You're here though, Nash. And so are those precious babies upstairs."

He looked at her, hard, then turned more fully to her and took both her hands in his. "I've had too many talks with myself. About making sure you get back in that SUV and hit the road, that you follow your big dreams."

Tell him. That something else was tugging at your heart and soul now. Something you didn't see coming. Was she just supposed to ignore that tug? Of course not. That was life—things changed.

But Nash Dawson also seemed very stuck in his own head, in the way he needed to look at this situation. That sending her off and away would heal something inside him.

Maybe she needed to let well enough alone and give him that. Go after her lifelong dream. Let the burgeoning one here just…be.

But she couldn't quite see doing that either.

Thing was, Nash was half this situation. And he wouldn't ask her to stay. In fact, he'd nudge her out the door to "bigger things."

Wendy looked at him, her heart thudding. For once, she actually heard her mother's voice: *What's bigger than love?* Andrea Watson was far from right about how she looked at her daughter's life and viewpoint. But love was powerful. And it had Wendy in its passionate grip.

Tell him. Say it.

"And if my big dreams detoured to the Dawson Brothers Cattle Ranch?" she blurted out. "To the three sleeping babies in the nursery? To the man sitting right here, a man I've loved my entire life?"

She could read so much in his eyes. But most of all: *This situation is complicated, Wendy.* Except it really wasn't. Not to her.

"Minus fifteen years," he whispered.

She shook her head. "You've always been in here, Nash," she said, pressing a hand to her heart. "I know what I want. And I want this. I want you."

She couldn't believe she'd said it. Come right out and said it. If there was a flicker of doubt about letting go of her long-held aspirations of far-off big cities, the fact that she'd been brave herself to tell Nash Dawson what she wanted, how she felt, was proof of what was burning in her heart now.

She wanted this. Him. This family.

"Wendy…" he said, looking so deeply into her eyes. She could see him thinking, hard. Assessing. Fighting with himself, maybe.

She leaned forward and kissed him. Tenderly, not passionately. Then she looked at him—and let everything she was feeling show there. She couldn't hide it anyway.

His shoulders dropped as if he'd stopped fighting himself. He lifted his hands to her face, looking at her with such depth of emotion, such passion. And then suddenly he was kissing her, his mouth fused to hers, his arms around her, pulling her closer, his hands in her hair.

Wendy closed her eyes as a ferocious desire overtook her. For so long she'd been denied this man. Now she was going to take him. And show him just how badly she did want him.

Not for a night either. She'd never be satisfied with that and she'd make sure he knew it loud and clear…

Chapter Twelve

Nowhere on Nash's bingo card for tonight was: passionately kiss Wendy Watson to the point that moments later she'd be straddling you on the sofa and all rational thought would leave your mind.

Her lips were so soft, her tongue roaming his mouth, her soft breath sometimes in his ear, sometimes on his neck as she trailed kisses along his collarbone. If he moved a muscle, he could quite possibly lose control, and he had every intention of prolonging this intense pleasure for as long as possible. He felt her hands slipping under his shirt, pressing against his chest, his nipples, her mouth once again on his neck. He groaned as she shifted, sliding up against the rock hard erection under his jeans.

Her soft cool hands were now unbuttoning his shirt, slipping it off, her mouth all over his chest now, dipping lower as she followed the trail of fine hairs to his belt buckle. She sat back—again sliding against his erection, and looked at him before undoing the belt and unsnapping his jeans, lowering the zipper. His head dropped back against the couch cushion in taut anticipation.

And then every muscle in his body stiffened as her hand reached into his boxer briefs and wrapped around him, moving up and down, up and down, her mouth once again on his.

He groaned and kissed her, his own hands finding their way under her shirt, then flinging it off. He opened his eyes to the treat of her lacy white bra, her lush breasts too hidden. He inched down the low-cut cups of the bra with his mouth and let his lips and tongue and hands explore the soft fullness, the rosy nipples. She arched against him, whispering his name, her breathy moans driving him wild with desire.

The big comfortable sofa felt suddenly tiny.

He picked her up and stood, the delighted and surprised expression on her beautiful face making him smile. He kissed her passionately as he carried her up the stairs and into the guest room.

She stiffened a bit in his arms when she clearly realized where he'd taken her. "You're not planning to say good night, are you?" she whispered into his ear as he laid her down on the bed.

Part of him knew he should do exactly that. A bigger part wanted this too much, needed it. And the fact that he was laying on top of Wendy in just her sexy bra and lacy underwear told him he'd come too far to stop now. That he hadn't shut down told him what he needed to know. That making love to Wendy was as right as it felt.

You've always been in here, Nash, she'd said and had pressed a hand to her heart. *I know what I want. And I want this. I want you.*

Those words had pushed something aside in him. Suddenly there was a little room where just days ago there had been none.

"It's the first room off the stairs and I couldn't get to a bed fast enough," he said very honestly.

She smiled and tightened her arms around his neck, pulling him down to her. He trailed kisses across the collarbone, down to her cleavage, slipping a hand behind her back to unclasp the bra and drop it over the edge of the bed.

The moment her bare chest was against his, he had to be closer to her, inside her. He reached for his wallet where he knew he had a condom. Wendy smiled seductively and grabbed it, setting the little foil-wrapped packet on the bedside table, and then nudging him over onto his back.

She straddled him again, shimmying his jeans from his hips and sliding them down his legs. He kicked them off. Then she bent and kissed and licked his chest, his nipples, down that line of hair again. She used her teeth to inch down his boxer briefs, and he groaned, gripping the sides of the mattress, and then setting his hands firmly on either side of her hips. She yanked off his underwear, and now all that separated them was her little white scrap of lace. He edged a finger in the waistband and slipped them down, his hand exploring every inch of her.

She moaned and writhed and he almost lost it. Her breath in his ear as she kissed his neck, her breasts against his bare chest...

She took the condom and in moments rolled it on

his throbbing erection. Then she slowly lowered herself onto him and rocked against him, her nails scraping just below his shoulders. He took in the beautiful view of her exquisite body, an unparalleled thrill shooting through him as she began to breathe harder, rock harder, her back arching before she clamped her mouth shut against what he knew was one hell of a scream.

And then he finally allowed himself to explode along with her. She dropped down against him, curling to his side. Nash wrapped an arm around her, holding her to him as they both worked to catch their breath.

"Amazing," he whispered, turning his head to her.

She opened her eyes and looked up at him. "Even more amazing than in my fantasies."

He smiled and pulled her even closer. She lay her head on his chest and he bent slightly to drop a kiss on her temple.

A calm peacefulness settled over him and his eyes drifted closed.

He didn't let himself think; he only *felt*. There was nowhere else he'd rather be than right here, in this bed, with this woman.

A faint but fussy cry woke Wendy, her eyes popping open in the darkness. She waited a beat to see if whoever had cried out would soothe himself back to sleep.

She didn't need to turn her head and reach out very gently to know that Nash was still beside her in bed. She was so filled up and happy that she'd known he was right there.

A warmth spread through her as she remembered

every detail of their night together. Starting with how forthright she'd been. Telling him how she felt.

I know what I want. And I want this. I want you. She smiled at the memory. *Good for you, Wendy Watson. You went after what you wanted—and now the man you've been in love with since you were twelve years old is lying naked beside you.*

She was smiling as she glanced at the window, at the sliver of moonlight coming through the slight opening in the curtains. She felt so happy, so fulfilled.

The faint cry came again, and she carefully got out of bed so as not to wake Nash. She couldn't resist just staring at him for a moment, this gorgeous specimen of man lying right here. The dream she'd held in her heart for so long had actually come true, and she still couldn't quite believe it, despite the evidence. She gave herself a tiny pinch and grinned that it hurt.

Wendy quickly slipped into her clothes and then hurried into the nursery. The fussy triplet was Dallas, his eyes wide open, his little legs kicking out.

"I've got you, bud," she said, reaching in to pick him up. *Bud.* She smiled, realizing that Nash sometimes called the triplets that.

With Dallas snuggled against her chest, she sat down in the glider chair by the window, glancing out at the stars visible. *If one wish came true, maybe the big one will,* she thought, resting her head against the sleepy baby's. The one where Nash would tell her that if she *really* meant it, if her dream had truly changed, if she now wanted *this*—this family, this life at the ranch—she would make him the happiest man on earth.

She shook her head at herself for getting a little fanciful. Going a little too far. She didn't even know how Nash felt about her. He cared about her, he was attracted to her—that wasn't in doubt. But was he falling in love?

Something told her that he wouldn't have even *kissed* her last night—let alone carried her upstairs in a way that felt like he was claiming her—if he didn't have big intentions. Like declaring his love. Like telling her that he wanted a future with her. A future with her as part of his family.

Her heart soared at just the thought.

Then again, Wendy had gotten hurt a few times over the years. Times she'd thought there was more going on than there actually was. Times when she'd been flat-out lied to because in the moment, the man had wanted sex and afterward was gone in the middle of the night. Times when someone else had come along who'd stolen her boyfriend away from her. Because his heart hadn't been Wendy's, after all. Those were rough experiences she'd gone through and gotten over, each leaving a little scar. Each making her afraid to try again.

But here she was, trying again—and this time with the man she could see herself married to. Sharing a life with. Perhaps in time, they'd have a baby and grow the family.

Yes, yes, yes, she thought. She wanted all that more than she wanted a big story or a view of the Empire State Building. She wanted a career in reporting, but she wanted Nash by her side as they pushed that triple stroller down Main Street together. Like Nash's grandmother had said, why couldn't she have both?

You know why, a small voice said from deep inside her.

Because Nash's feelings for her were a mystery. She cuddled Dallas closer, suddenly worried. Nash was a good guy. The very best of guys. But that didn't mean he wouldn't hurt her—even if he didn't mean to. Good guys could get carried away by the moment too. By sexual desire and a very willing participant. The morning light had a way of changing things.

She bit her lip and stared out the window, pushing aside the curtain to look at the stars. There were so many tonight that they had to be a good sign.

Another cry came from the cribs—she was pretty sure it was Ryder. *Huh*, she thought, her smile returning. She could tell who was fussing in one note. But just as she got up to head over, Nash appeared in the doorway and he seemed to freeze at the sight of her.

As though he hadn't expected to see her there. Holding his baby nephew. In the middle of the night. Like she didn't belong there or something.

Oh, hell, she thought, her heart plummeting as she was very aware of the change in him, his eyes, his expression, his body language.

Something had gone wrong. Something about seeing her in the nursery with Dallas had affected him—exactly how she wasn't sure, but it did not seem to be good.

Instead of looking at her the way he had just a few

hours ago, as if he couldn't get enough of her, there was awkward silence.

He went to the crib and picked up Ryder. "Huh. He feels warm." He put the back of his hand to the baby's forehead. Definitely hot. He held Ryder against his bare chest, giving his back gentle rubs in a circular motion. Ryder was making little fussy sounds. Nash paced the room, not quite looking at Wendy. "I hope you're not sick, bud," he said, concern etched in his handsome face.

Bud. Her heart pinched.

With his worry about Ryder, this certainly wasn't the time to ask about *them*. About what had changed. And something had.

She sucked in a breath and carefully returned Dallas to his crib. The baby moved his head, his arm shooting up by his ear, where it settled. His lip quirked, his eyes remaining closed. He was definitely asleep again.

She turned to Nash. He was standing by the window now, his gaze down on the baby in his arms.

"What can I do to help?" she asked.

He looked up at her, then back at Ryder. "I've got this," he said with slight awkward smile again. "I'll stay up with him until he falls back to sleep. You go get some rest."

Rest? That wasn't happening. She'd lay in bed and speculate herself into a knot of worry.

Dammit.

She turned to go, her heart cracking.

"Wendy," he said.

She turned, hope burgeoning.

"I'm…sorry," he said, holding her gaze for just a moment before looking away, then down at the baby in his arms. His tone was suddenly a little stony. Resolute. "I thought…"

Oh, no. No, no, no.

Now her heart was cracking and her legs felt shaky. *You thought you could but you can't.* What else was there to say?

She was certainly too choked up to say anything herself. And he looked so pained that she just wanted to let him be.

Whatever it was that had flipped a switch in Nash and had him a million miles away from her, they would not be talking about it now.

But she knew he was saying goodbye. After their first kiss, he'd been settled on nothing happening between them. Then something had, something big.

She could hear the goodbye in his voice.

She wasn't willing to let him go though. There was too much between them—love and connection and chemistry and promise. And a *family*.

He needed time, and she would give it to him. At the moment, she had no choice anyway. Ryder had a fever and the baby had to come first.

Wendy had always stood up for what she believed— and wanted. And she wasn't stopping now.

Chapter Thirteen

At close to 4:00 a.m., Nash was walking a fussy Ryder around the house. The baby had fallen asleep in Nash's arms twice during the past few hours, but had awakened, red-faced and crying. He still felt warm, but his fever was borderline. Nash had given him OTC fever reducer, which helped Ryder sleep, but that hadn't lasted long.

Nash moved over to the fireplace and stood in front of the mantel, staring at a photo of his brother. It had been a different photo of Ethan in the upstairs hallway, when he'd woken in the guest room to a cry and realized Wendy wasn't beside him—that had stopped him in his tracks. And changed everything for him. Something had closed down inside him. Then he'd come upon Wendy in the nursery and felt himself completely close off to her. Like he had any right to do that after he'd slept with her.

Dammit.

He'd hurt her—he'd seen that in her expression, heard it in her voice. And then two hours ago, when Ryder had woken the second time, Wendy had come into the nursery to say that she'd be happy to relieve

Nash so he could get some sleep. For a moment, as he'd looked at her in the doorway, beautiful Wendy, such concern in her eyes—for Ryder and him—he'd wanted to get up and go to her and wrap her in his arms. To feel the way he had much earlier in the night.

But everything was different now.

He'd told Wendy he was okay and she'd nodded, then waited just a few seconds and left. He'd felt like such a jerk. But he had no idea how to fix things. Not then, not now. He should have left well enough alone by not kissing her again. Because they'd taken things to the next level.

"That's your daddy," he whispered to Ryder as he stared at his favorite photo of Ethan. His brother was sitting on the sofa at his house in Cheyenne, holding all three infants. How small they'd been just six months ago—two days old in the picture.

Had he ever seen a bigger smile on her brother's face? Maybe only Ethan's wedding day rivaled the look on his face in that photo.

Such happiness. Pride. Joy.

And Nash had been so unfair to him out of misplaced, unfair resentment. For years, berating Ethan for his "screwed up priorities." Putting *himself* first.

Without Nash realizing he himself had been doing the same thing. Putting himself over his brother by demanding. Demanding Ethan give back, commit more, be part of the family he'd left behind.

"Your daddy was a superstar," he whispered to Ryder.

And Nash had tried to dim his star because he was thinking about himself about the ranch and not Ethan. Unable to see the situation from any angle but his own.

The Dawson Brothers Cattle Ranch went through some hard times, particularly in the years when Ethan was up-and-coming as a rodeo participant. His brother had contributed financially to the ranch when he started winning big, and though Nash had appreciated it, he'd still wanted his brother to give his time and attention to the ranch. To the family. Ethan had been the older brother, the one Nash always wanted to turn to, but his brother had never been around.

I let your father down, Nash thought, voice low and broken, the shame spiraling in his gut. *But I won't let you and your brothers down. Or Wendy. She needs to go after her lifelong dream. If she goes for it and finds it's really not what she wants anymore, then fine. But she has to go for it, right?*

That was pretty much where Nash was and had been when he'd come into the nursery earlier and found Wendy holding Dallas. When he'd awakened in the guest room—surprised to discover he was alone, then heard her voice and realized a baby must have gotten up and she'd gone to check on him. Then that photo in the hallway between the guest room and the nursery had changed everything. He'd stopped and stared at it, at Ethan at seventeen on that bronc, and Nash had been seized by sorrow—and then by such longing. That he could undo the past. Change that last conversation. Celebrate his brother's goals instead of dumping on them.

And seeing Wendy in the nursery, holding Dallas—his mind had immediately gone back to the photo. Ethan had come in third in a major event and he thought it meant he was on his way. He wanted to practice more, completely stop working at the ranch before school—and he'd long stopped helping out after school so that he could use those hours for bronc-riding practice. Fifteen-year-old Nash had had to give up any extracurriculars, including the 4-H Club, to pick up the slack.

Strange thing was, even then, when Nash had been furious at this brother, he was still proud. Proud of his brother's skills, that he'd won a medal so young, that he was on his way, but very upset that the ranch wasn't a thought in Ethan's mind. That he was going to leave them all high and dry when he should be pitching in.

They'd had words then too, Nash making sure Ethan knew that third wasn't *first* place, and maybe when he won the big prize, then he could ditch his responsibilities. Ethan's face had fallen. Nash felt like a jerk but he'd been unable to stop himself.

That was pretty much how things had always gone between him and his brother. Even when Ethan had won a first-place prize, and he slowly stopped coming home at all if a rodeo took him far away. Even for major celebrations and family events. He'd missed their father's surgery for a competition, no matter that their mom had insisted their dad would want Ethan to compete, not sit in the waiting room. Nash had been livid that Ethan chose the rodeo over their dad. He should be home, he'd kept thinking. He should be beside him and his mother and grandmother in the waiting room.

And now Ethan was gone.

And the sight of Wendy, where she *didn't* belong—the way he saw it—here, at the ranch, just like at the Watson Dairy. Holding a baby when her dream was her *career*. All she'd been through with her mother, fighting for herself the way Ethan had tried to fight for himself with Nash. He'd stared at Wendy in the nursery and knew it was all wrong. That she wasn't supposed to be here.

And something in him had gone stone-cold about the two of them romantically.

He wanted Wendy in New York or LA. Her byline on big stories. He wanted to think of her in an apartment on the thirtieth floor with a balcony facing the river or a bridge. That was what she used to talk about. Not marriage and family. Her life suddenly about a ranch and three babies. Even thinking of her staying with him and the triplets at the ranch felt to Nash like he'd be taking something away from her and saddling her with the very life she'd never wanted.

He loved his life. But this had always been his dream. And raising Ethan's boys let him give back to his brother, make good on one promise at least.

But if he tried to explain all this again, she'd argue that he wasn't listening. That her dream had changed. She'd never said she didn't want to be an investigative journalist though. Only that she'd fallen for him and the triplets and wanted them just as much.

He couldn't let her give up on herself. He couldn't.

"I care about her too much for that, Ryder," he whispered to the baby. He stood there, in front of the photo of Ethan with his three infants on his lap, proud, happy father, and his eyes misted with tears.

In a couple of hours, his parents and grandmother would be coming by to pick up Dallas and Callum;

they'd been planning to take all three babies into town for breakfast with their grandparents' club—once a month, their group took over the coffee shop in the early morning with babies and toddlers and preschoolers. But since Ryder was under the weather, Nash would keep him home.

Ryder's eyes were drooping. Nash gently rocked him, then took the photo of Ethan from the mantel and brought it over to the sofa. He sat down carefully, nestling the baby in the crook of his arm, then set the photo on the coffee table. He needed to remember that this—his brother, the promise Nash had made to do right by these babies, would be the driving force of his life. Not his love life.

And if there was one way he could make peace with letting down Ethan in that last conversation, it was to let Wendy go. To soar. To fly. To champion her the way he hadn't championed his brother.

He glanced down at his nephew. Fast asleep. He touched a hand to Ryder's forehead. He was less hot, but still warm. "Your Uncle Nash will always be here for you and your brothers," he whispered.

Once his parents left with Dallas and Callum, he'd go talk to Wendy. He'd explain himself—beyond an "I'm sorry." Beyond "I thought..."

She deserved more.

She deserved the world. And he'd have to let her go for that.

Wendy had barely slept at all. Her phone rang at just before 6:00 a.m. and she grabbed it off the bedside table. Could it be Nash reporting in about how Ryder was doing? Maybe he was at the urgent care?

Maybe he was calling to ask her to come to his bedroom, that he couldn't live without her another second...

No—it was her sister. A video call.

She clicked Join, and Tess's crumpling face, with red-rimmed eyes and tears pooling, appeared on the little screen. Oh, no.

Wendy's heart started pounding and she sat up in bed. "Tess, what happened? Are Mom and Dad okay?"

Tess sniffled. "They're okay, sorry, yes. It's me who's not."

Oh, hell. This had to be about Braydon.

Tears streamed down Tess's cheeks. "Braydon broke up with me. He said he knew for absolutely sure that he didn't want children and that it wouldn't be right to stay together when he knew how much I wanted to be a mother." She broke down in sobs.

Wendy's heart was clenching for her sister. "I'm so sorry, Tess. I'll be right there, okay. I'm throwing my stuff in a bag and coming right over. Fifteen minutes."

Her sister continued to cry and then broke the connection. Wendy jumped out of bed and gathered all her things, stuffing them in her duffel. She hurried into the bathroom, washed her face and brushed her teeth, then threw her toiletries in the bag. After making sure she had everything since she wasn't sure she'd be back at all, Wendy went to find Nash.

He was in the kitchen, pouring coffee. For a moment, at the sight of him, all she could think was *I love you, I love you, I love you.* But a second later, reality set in. Her sister needed her.

Ryder was in the gently rocking baby bouncer by the table, gnawing on a chew toy. He turned as she stopped in the doorway, his gaze on the duffel bag hanging over her shoulder.

"Braydon broke up with Tess. I'm on my way to the farm now. I'll likely stay for a few days before…" She couldn't bear to stay the words. *Leaving town.*

He grimaced. "I'm so sorry for her—and him. I wouldn't give up on Braydon though. He just might need some time to come around."

Time. Same with you? she wanted to ask.

How did you know when someone just needed time or if that was it, decision made? How much time did you give *yourself* to wait and hope?

She inwardly sighed. Then she realized how quiet it was in the house and looked around. The kitchen playpen by the window was empty. She turned to look at the one in the living room and it was also baby-free. Only Ryder seemed home at the moment.

As she was turning back around, her gaze caught on a framed photo on the coffee table. Ethan Dawson with the newborn triplets nestled on his lap. Gosh, they were so little.

An understanding dawned. Nash had been looking at the photograph. Probably all night. His last conversation with his brother, just a day before Ethan had died, had Nash tied in knots. *I understand*, she wanted to say. *All of it. Every heartbreaking, compli-*

cated piece of it. I just wish you'd hear me. The way you used to.

That was the issue. He couldn't anymore.

She'd been planning to fight for him. Fight for them. But right now, maybe with her sister's broken heart foremost in her mind, she realized it was a losing battle.

"My parents and grandmother took Dallas and Callum into town for their grandparents club," he said. "I'm hanging with Ryder until he stops being cranky. He doesn't feel warm any more but something might be up. Maybe he's coming down with something."

She bit her lip and nodded. "I wish I could say goodbye to them."

A little voice said, *Guess you'll have to come back then, won't you?* At least there was that. She couldn't just leave Bear Ridge in a few days without a proper goodbye to all three Dawson boys. Whom she loved.

She blinked away that stinging feeling that told her she was on the verge of tears.

"Well," she said. "I'll be writing the story from the farm. I'll send it to you for approval, as discussed."

As discussed. Business-speak. Professional. That was the way it had to be for now.

He nodded, then faced her fully, looking directly at her. "Wendy. Again, I'm sorry. I thought that— but—I…"

Ryder let out a little wail and flailed his arms. Nash seemed to snap to attention and hurried over to the baby, picking him up out of the bouncer and soothing him.

She stayed where she was. "I hope you feel better, sweet Ryder," she cooed to the baby. Then she looked at Nash, the man she loved, and turned to go.

When the front door closed behind her, she cried all the way to her car.

Chapter Fourteen

Wendy was curled up on one end of the love seat in her sister's cabin at the Watson Dairy, Tess at the other, a plush throw over her and a box of tissues on the arm rest. Wendy wrapped her hands around her mug of coffee, wishing things could magically be different for both of them. She'd arrived about ten minutes ago, and her sister had just stopped crying.

"We'd been arguing back and forth all night," Tess said. "We fell asleep on the sofa for a few hours. I woke up around five a.m. and went out to check on Mo, one of the calves, and when I came back, Braydon was sitting up right where you are now. And I had this feeling something had changed for him. He stood and said that he was one hundred percent sure he didn't want to have children, now or ever, and he was saying goodbye for my own good." Her eyes welled.

"Oh, Tess," Wendy said, her heart twisting. "I'm so sorry."

Tess's face crumpled and she swiped under her eyes. "And then he left. Just walked out the door. I ran after him and called his name and he just kept going. I even ran after his pickup like an idiot. Until I just stopped and cried in the middle of the driveway. Dad came running out to find out what was going on, and I broke down and told him everything. He actually cried—he felt so bad for both Braydon and for me. And then I called you, so he waited till your car pulled in to give us some privacy to talk."

Wendy's heart was in tatters for her sister, but she felt for Braydon too. He was in a lot of pain over the subject of having children.

A knock came at the door. Tess jumped up, clearly hoping it was Braydon, back to say he'd gotten as far as his apartment in town and realized he couldn't live without Tess in his life.

But it was their mother, and Wendy braced herself for Andrea Watson to say the wrong things. Then again, she tended to be kinder when it came to Tess, who'd always been so devoted to the farm.

Their mom was holding a covered tray in two hands. "I brought breakfast. I know you probably have no appetite, honey," she said to Tess. "But sometimes comfort food is just what the doctor ordered. I have scrambled eggs, bacon, bagels and cream cheese, and those raspberry and white chocolate scones you like."

That was nice. Very nice.

"I don't think I can eat but thanks, Mom," Tess said.

Same here, Wendy thought. She hadn't told anyone about her own broken heart. When she'd arrived, Tess and their dad had been sitting on the porch steps of the house, both looking stricken. Wendy had gone into big-sister mode, pulling Tess into a hug, and their dad had patted Wendy on the shoulder and let her take over.

Andrea set the tray on the coffee table, then sat on the swivel chair adjacent to the love seat. "I hope you don't mind that your dad filled me in, sweetheart." She took Tess's hand and held it. "I know how much you love Braydon and I do think he'll come around, but he'll likely need to talk to a good therapist. Someone who can really help him work out his feelings."

Wendy's mouth almost dropped open. Her mother had always been dismissive of therapy. She'd say that most people could work out their problems by talking to those who loved and cared about them, friends or relatives and getting different perspectives—not to a paid stranger.

What her mom didn't know was that Wendy had gone to therapy for over a year when she'd first moved away from the farm. Despite her dad's and sister's support, her mother's issues with Wendy's choices had bothered her to the point that she knew she needed to talk to someone completely impartial—and yes, paid to listen and give good advice because of their credentials and experience. Her weekly visits had done her a lot of good.

"I wish he would," Tess said. "I've suggested it. But he keeps saying he feels how he feels. I'd tell him that the point is helping him see that he *doesn't* have to feel that way, but he'd just get angry and walk away."

Wendy nodded, feeling so bad for the two of them. "The two of you have been broken up for what—an hour? That man does love you, Tess. And once he sits with the pain he's causing himself—and you—I think he'll start wishing he did look at things differently. And maybe that's where he'll start shifting his mindset."

"I think Wendy is right," their mom said with a warm nod.

Huh. Wendy glanced at her mom and gave her an appreciative look, which her mother returned.

Tess dabbed at her eyes. "I'll try not to think about it too much but I'm going to be so distracted. And I really should get to the barn and handle the milking."

"You stay right here," Wendy said. "I'll take care of the milking. I've got you, okay?"

Tess sniffled and nodded, pulling the throw more fully over her.

"And Dad and I will help as much as we can too," their mom said. They'd half-retired this past year—only half because they loved working the dairy rather than because Wendy wasn't around. That had always given her some comfort.

Tess swiped under her eyes "Thank you both. I don't know what I'd do without you."

Wendy got up and gave Tess a hug.

"I'll stay here for a while," Andrea said, then looked up at Wendy. "If you need help in the barn, just text."

Wendy nodded and headed out. The sky was overcast, which suited her mood—gloomy. But the familiarity of Watson Dairy was suddenly a comfort when usually it was such a source of tension for her. She used to think of the farm as representing everything standing in the way of her and her goals. But part of her would always love this place, remembering how she and Tess loved the cows and giggled at their funny-looking udders. How they jumped on and off hay bales. How they ran around the pastures and came home filthy.

She somehow managed a smile at some of those sweet memories.

The farm had a milking system, which the family—and the cows—appreciated. Wendy changed from her sneakers into a pair of calf-high rubber boots in the entrance to the barn, glad she was already in worn jeans and a long-sleeved T-shirt, her hair in a ponytail. She got the first group of their small herd of thirty-two cows ready to go, happy to see her dad come join her.

Davis Watson was always a source of comfort.

"How's Tess?" he asked, his green eyes full of concern.

Without remotely meaning to, Wendy burst into tears.

"Oh, no, honey, I'm sorry. It's hard to see someone you love hurting."

Wendy swiped at her eyes. "I'm actually crying over myself, unfortunately," she managed to say between sniffles.

She told her dad everything. Including that she and Nash had *kissed and then some*, as she put it. But that it was over now; he was all tied up in knots over the loss of his brother and last time he'd spoken to Ethan. He'd shared a bit more of the gist of their conversation. Her heart clenched whenever she thought about it.

"He looks at the idea of me staying in Bear Ridge, changing diapers and letting the herd out to graze, as some kind of slap in the face to Ethan's memory. I understand how he feels. But I'm not Ethan."

Her dad nodded. "That's rough, hon. Seems to me that both Nash and Braydon need to find some peace before they can move on. Or lack of peace."

Wendy turned to her dad. "Lack of peace? What do you mean?"

"I don't think Braydon wants to lose Tess. And I don't think Nash wants to lose you. Once that sinks in, really sinks in, they'll both have to deal with their uncomfortable feelings about what's making them push you and Tess away. And once they get through that, they'll be back."

Wendy felt hopeful for the first time since Nash had said *I'm sorry, but*. "But what if neither of them is willing to deal with those uncomfortable feelings? What if they just bury all that?"

"Can't do that for too long," her father said. "Without going completely mad."

"Thanks, Dad," she said, and wrapped her arms around him. "You always know just what to say to make me feel better."

"That's my job," he said, kissing the top of her head. "How'd your mom do when she brought over breakfast?"

Wendy smiled. She knew exactly what her dad meant. "She did great. Even surprised *me*."

Davis Watson laughed. But just as her father hadn't been able to help her mom see Wendy differently all these years, she worried that nothing would change the minds of Braydon and Nash.

"Let's give both guys a little time—and distance," he said. "And see."

Wendy brightened at that. Something structured, not that *a little time* was defined in the slightest. She'd help out at the farm, be there for Tess and she'd write her article. And then when it was time to go, she'd make some decisions. The only thing she knew for sure was that she wouldn't leave Bear Ridge without making sure Nash Dawson knew how she felt. She'd made it clear already, but if all she had was her voice, she'd use it.

Right now, Watson Dairy needed her and she was right here, finding great comfort in helping.

Nash had to get out of the house, had to get away from the ranch, where suddenly he was reminded of Wendy with every step. Just being on the property called up memories. In the barn, he'd suddenly been struck by a memory of when they were eight years old and doing their math work sheets up in the hayloft. On the trail by the creek, when they were ten and looking for frogs. Out in the backyard, when they were twelve and she'd stay for dinner and she was enchanted by fireflies they'd tried to catch in their hands.

And in the house, now, she was everywhere. How she'd so carefully hold a triplet while giving a bottle. Her laugh while playing peekaboo. Sitting at the kitchen table, giving one of the boys their jar of oatmeal and peaches.

The living room got him the worst though. The sofa, where they'd kissed last night, so passionately that just thinking about it made his knees weak. And the guest room, where he found himself drawn to right now, Ryder in his arms.

The baby was wide-awake and over his hours-long mystery illness, thankfully no fever, color back in his cheeks. His pediatrician thought it might have been a passing stomach bug that had come and gone.

Now Nash stood in the doorway of the room where they'd made love. The room Wendy had stayed in, now empty of her things. The bed made, no sign she'd ever been there.

His head, his heart, his stomach felt hollow.

Everything felt wrong without her around.

Because you care about her, he thought as he carried Ryder into the nursery to get him changed and ready to go pick up his brothers in town. *Because you know you're doing the right thing by letting her go.*

With Ryder all set, Nash settled him in the stroller and headed out to this SUV. The sight of the one baby in the stroller meant for three only compounded how wrong everything felt, how upside down.

But he had a plan. He was meeting his parents at the coffee shop, then he'd take the triplets to the park and they'd watch the ducks, one of their favorite things to do. He'd focus on his life's mission—the triplets, raising them, loving them, taking care of them. Balancing that with running the ranch and keeping it successful. Watching over his parents and grandmother. His life was busy and full and he'd known when he first acknowledged that he had feelings for Wendy that he had no room in that life—or his heart—for a relationship. He'd get his head back where it should be and he'd be okay.

Twenty minutes later, he stopped at the coffee shop to pick up Callum and Ryder, chatted with his parents and Gram and their grandparent group for a bit, itching to get away. His dad came out with him to help get all three babies in their rear-facing car seats.

"You okay?" his dad asked as he buckled Callum's harness. He leaned back out of the SUV and looked at Nash, studying him. "You look…unhappy."

I am. Very. "I'm fine, Dad," he lied, trying to get a reassuring smile on his face. "Just got some things on my mind."

His father tilted his head. "Anything you want to talk about?" The concern in his dad's voice almost broke Nash.

He put an arm around his father's shoulders and said he'd work it out, no worries, and his dad's expression seemed to brighten, so Nash felt better about not saddling the man with his problems. His dad would tell his mom that Nash looked…sad, and then they'd be worried and spend the rest of the day talking about it amongst themselves, coming over with food to check on him. Nash didn't want to put that on them. And he wouldn't be able to talk about what was bothering him. Just like he never could talk about Ethan with them.

How ashamed they'd be of him if they knew about that last phone conversation.

The extent to which Nash had resented Ethan's choices.

He'd hate to disappoint them after they'd been through so much.

Nash gave his dad a hug, then watched him go back inside the coffee shop and sit down at the table with his mom and grandmother. Part of him wished he *could* run in and unload. Tell them how awful he felt, what a mess he'd made of things.

His relationship with Ethan. His relationship with Wendy.

But instead he sucked in a breath and drove off toward the park down the street. As he pulled into a spot, the first thing he saw was Braydon's family feedstore across the lot. In fact, there was Braydon himself, pulling a dolly containing several bags of feed out to a pickup. He was a good distance away, but he could see that Braydon looked miserable.

Like he clearly did if his dad had noticed.

He got the triplets out of their seats and back in the stroller and wheeled them toward the park's entrance, already feeling slightly better. He had his boys with him. Ryder seemed absolutely fine now. And the day had turned gorgeous after an overcast morning.

Nash had some birdseed for the ducks in a baggie in the stroller basket. The triplets would laugh their heads off at watching the ducks peck at the seeds, and for a little while Nash would feel restored. That was the plan anyway. To try to get his equilibrium back.

He pushed the stroller down the path, past the tennis courts and the fountain in the center, and headed for the pond. There was a footbridge just wide enough for the stroller, and he followed it until he got to the other side where the ducks congregated. There were benches and trees and a coffee truck that he might pay a visit to on the way out.

He wheeled the stroller close to the pond so that the triplets would have a good view, Callum already laughing at the antics of the ducks, two zooming into the water and hopping up onto a mini island of stones in the center.

"I know that laugh," said a familiar voice.

He whirled around to find Wendy, her arm linked around her sister's. Tess looked just like Braydon had across the lot. Absolutely miserable.

A lot of that going round these days.

Wendy didn't look much happier.

She whispered something to Tess, who sat down on a bench nearby and watched the ducks. Wendy came forward. "At least I get to say goodbye to the triplets." She kneeled down and gazed at each of them, her expression so sad it deepened the crack in his heart.

"You're leaving town today?" he asked, the thought of her back in Cheyenne both comforting and painful.

"No," she said, standing up. "I'm staying for a few days. Tess is hurting and I'm going to take over her duties at the farm so she can just cry if she needs to."

He nodded. "If you need help—"

"I've got it," she said. "I grew up doing farm chores and it's second nature even if I've been away from the everyday of it for seven years now. Plus, I like talking to the cows. They just listen."

Instead of argue. He understood.

"Just so there's no question, Nash, since you didn't

exactly finish what you were saying this morning. You said, 'I'm sorry. I thought—' You thought...what, exactly?"

He looked away for a second. *She deserves to fully understand. Try to explain what's going on in your thick head.*

"I thought that how I feel about you was all that mattered," he finally said. "That I could just start with that..." He paused and glanced away. "And then in the middle of the night, when you were in the nursery, I passed a photo of my brother on the wall upstairs and I stood there staring at it. Seventeen years old. His first third-place win. I couldn't look away from the joy on Ethan's face. It's the joy I used to see on your face when you'd talk about the career you planned for yourself."

Her green eyes got misty and she touched a hand to her heart. "That means so much to me, Nash. That it means that much to *you*. But I told you that I want to share your life with you at the ranch. With you and the triplets."

"I'm not discounting that. That you feel that way too. I just can't live with you giving up your dreams when you're so close, Wendy."

She was quiet for a moment. She turned to look at where her sister sat, Tess's attention on the ducks. Then Wendy looked at the triplets, her expression turning so wistful and sad again that he wished he could pull her into his arms. And apologize. But he knew he was doing the right thing by letting her go.

She turned her attention back to him, lifting her chin. "Well, since you're not willing to take what I say at face value, I won't take what you say at face value. I think something else is keeping you from welcoming me into your life. Into the triplets' lives."

He felt himself stiffen. He knew, in that moment, that if that was true, he didn't want to know what it was.

The collar of his shirt felt tight. "I'd better get the triplets back home for their nap," he said, forgetting in this very uncomfortable moment that she was well aware of the babies' nap schedule and they weren't due for a while.

"At least I have that confirmed," she said, her voice cracking.

"All I know is how I feel, Wendy."

She sucked in a breath and then moved over to the stroller again. She kneeled down, a warm smile overtaking her beautiful face. "Hey, guys. I loved spending time with the three of you. I'm going to write an article all about you. Maybe Uncle Nash will read it to you. My heart will be in every word." She touched a finger to each baby's cheek, then stood and turned and hurried back over to the bench. Her sister got up and eyed him for a moment, then they walked away. Fast.

His heart was pounding in his chest to the point that he had to sit down. He dropped onto the bench beside the stroller, then turned and watched part of his heart disappear around a curve in the path.

Chapter Fifteen

Two days had passed since Wendy ran into Nash in the park. She'd spent her time working at the farm, Tess often beside her and trying to distract herself with manual labor or just sitting and watching the goats. Every now and then, the adorable calves got a laugh out of Tess, but she was so broken-hearted that she'd tear up a moment later. Wendy had shared her own heartache with Tess, told her everything, and if there was a silver lining in all this, it was that the two of them grew even closer. They had *a lot* in common these days.

Right now, in the late afternoon, Tess was mucking out the goat stalls while Wendy was in the pasture leading the cows farther out. She'd given up on trying not to think about Nash since for the past two days she'd been writing the article about him and the triplets in her head, often her process before she sat down at her laptop. The "interviews" would play back in her mind and she'd think of all the notes she'd taken, but the heart of the story would come from inside her. She'd start it tonight, get a first draft out, then let it sit till the light of dawn, when she could revise and edit and polish with a more discerning eye. Once she was happy with it, she'd send it to Nash. He'd make whatever changes he wanted, send it back, and then that would be that.

Her reason for being in Bear Ridge would be officially over—on a professional level.

She didn't feel ready to leave her sister, not when Tess was so raw. Once she did send the article to her boss, she'd ask for a couple days' vacation and she was sure Janna would approve that. Then she'd figure out her next steps. She'd go back to Cheyenne, back to her life, but she was hardly surprised that she wasn't excited by that, wasn't brimming with anticipation at what might be coming next. A promotion. Bigger stories. A chance to show her bosses what she was truly capable of. And then she'd have the kind of clips she could show the big-city media outlets. She'd be on her way.

The problem was that she no longer wanted to go. Maybe it was her own heartache talking. Maybe once she was back in Cheyenne, at the *Gazette*, which had always filled her up, in her tiny studio apartment, which she loved because it was her own place, working on those important stories, she'd be back to her old self.

Except how did she ignore that she wanted something different? That she'd experienced love—to the depth that she felt it for Nash. That she'd shared in his family life to the point that she knew she wanted that for herself.

"Smart of you to move the herd out here and give the front pasture a break."

Wendy turned around at the sound of her mother's

voice. She'd been so lost in thought she hadn't heard her approach.

"The grass is patchy in a lot of spots by the barn," Wendy said absently, her gaze on the cows, grazing away where the grass was abundant.

She could feel her mom studying her, and it made her itchy. She feigned more interest in the cows than she felt at the moment.

"I made butternut squash soup—I know how much you love it. Want to come back to the house for some? I also have half a loaf of sourdough left."

Butternut squash soup and a slice of homemade sourdough sounded very comforting right now. "Sure. And thanks." She and her mother might not ever really talk, ever work out their issues, but at least they were both trying.

Her mother smiled and they headed for the farmhouse. "So when do you think you'll be heading home to Cheyenne?"

"Probably in two days," she said, daring a glance at her mother and bracing herself for the barrage of criticism.

But Andrea Watson just nodded. "It's been so nice having you home," she said, giving Wendy's hand a squeeze. "But I know you have to get back. You must miss the newsroom."

That was a nice surprise. But Wendy couldn't seem to find her voice. *I do but I miss Nash and the triplets more.* She couldn't imagine confiding in her mom about where things stood with Nash. That what she wanted most of all was for him to ask her to stay and share his life and help him raise the triplets. That no such offer would be coming.

They walked in silence as they headed up the porch steps into the house. Wendy could smell that delicious soup the moment she stepped inside. In the kitchen, she eyed the big pot on the back burner.

"You cooked, I'll serve," Wendy said.

Her mom smiled and sat down at the table. "So have you started the article yet? About Nash and the triplets?"

Wendy shook her head, then ladled out two bowls of the fragrant orange soup. She brought them to the table, then cut two slices of the bread. "I'm going to write a draft tonight."

"I'd love to read it when you're done," her mom said.

Wendy just nodded since her mother wouldn't say anything after, just like always. And it would hurt Wendy's feelings, just like always.

They ate and chatted about the farm, Wendy sharing that she had new favorites among the cows.

"I already made room in the newest Wendy book for the article," Andrea Watson said, buttering the bread.

"The Wendy book?" She assumed her mom meant the scrapbook she'd made for each daughter back when they started preschool. It was full of firsts—the first time Wendy had written her name, artwork with blue suns and people with green faces. Pictures of Wendy with the herd over the years. The first time she'd milked a cow when she was six, milk more on the floor and all over her than in the bucket. At some point, in high school, Wendy had realized that none of her clippings from the school newspapers or the *Bear Ridge Free Weekly* made the scrapbook and she'd stopped looking at it altogether.

"The scrapbook I keep of your articles," her mom said. "I'll show you."

Wendy stared at her mother in confusion as Andrea got up and went to the desk at the far window, where her mother always sat to do the farm books. She opened one of the bottom drawers and pulled out a pile of scrapbooks. Then a few more.

The scrapbook of my articles, Wendy repeated to herself, tilting her head as her mother carried the stack over to the table.

Wendy opened the top one and gasped. She flipped pages and pages of her articles from middle school and high school and the free weekly. Three scrapbooks' worth. The next one was from her first job at the *Brewer Daily News*—her entire history of clips fit on two pages even though she'd worked there for over a year because they'd been very short articles about school board meetings or the Brewer High School's cross-country team's times in their championship win. Her next three jobs as a reporter were in two more scrapbooks, every article she'd written.

"But how—?" she asked, looking at her mother, her eyes getting all teary. "How did you even find these?"

"I know how to Google," Andrea Watson said with a soft smile. "I used to do that to feel a connection to you when you were far away. Even just forty minutes away in Brewer in your first apartment. I'd find a clip online and print it out." She brought over the final scrapbook and patted the blue floral cover. "This one here is from your last job and current job at the *Gazette*."

Wendy was so touched she couldn't speak, let alone even move to open the cover. She sucked in a breath and cleared her throat and opened the scrapbook. All her latest articles, including the one that had gotten her the attention of the *Gazette* editors. There were her Good Samaritan features, short and sweet. And the very last one—the one about the ten-year-old girl who'd rescued her elderly neighbor's cat. Wendy herself hadn't even seen that published in the paper or online. She'd filed that story the day she left for Bear Ridge.

Which meant that her mother looked for Wendy's work *every day*.

"Oh, Mom," she said, tears slipping down her cheeks. She got up and put her arms out, and Andrea Watson got up too. They hugged. "I had no idea. I thought you hated anything to do with my career. But you've been keeping a history since I was in sixth grade."

Her mom wiped away her own tears and nodded. "Just because I was angry and wanted you at the farm, didn't mean I wasn't still proud—in my own way. Your dad's been telling me for years that I should show you these scrapbooks but I'd always shake my head and say they were for me. But last night, your dad said something that struck me. He said, 'Gosh, we raised a good girl in Wendy. The way she's tending to Tess and the farm when it's clear she has her own broken heart.' And I gasped and said, 'What?' And he said, 'Come on, you can't tell?' And I felt so ashamed in that moment, at how little I actually know my own daughter that I got out these scrapbooks and read every last article. I did *a lot* of thinking last night."

Wendy stared at her mother in absolute shock. She wasn't surprised her father had been able to tell before today that his older daughter was *also* heartbroken; she and her dad had always been close. Of course he'd known before she told him.

"I'm sorry I never told you how much I admire you, Wendy. I was too focused on myself and what I thought—instead of actually thinking about you. I'm sorry, honey. I'm very sorry."

Wendy was so moved that she couldn't speak for a second. She pulled her mom into another hug, tears streaming down her face. "It means so much to me to hear you say all that."

They stood and hugged for a good long while.

"I want you to know that whatever's going on," her mom said, "Whatever went wrong between you and Nash—I think it'll work itself out. Just like I believe it will with Tess and Braydon."

"I'm not so sure about me and Nash," Wendy said, sitting back down. "He feels how he feels."

"I thought I did too," Andrea said with a smile. "And if I can change, *anyone* can."

"Oh, Mom," she said, grabbing her mother's hand as hope filled her. "Thank you for saying that."

"This is what I know now, Wendy. Wherever your heart is, *that's* the right place for you to be. All these years, I didn't understand that. And right now, your heart seems to be with the farm because of Tess. I'm grateful for that. But in two days, when that same heart leads you back to Cheyenne and then to Los Angeles or even a European city, I'll feel the same way."

Wendy felt some very old roughened cracks fill up in her heart and soul. She didn't know if she'd have a future with Nash and the triplets. But she did know she had her mom back.

"I think *Nash's* heart will surprise us all," her mom added, giving Wendy's hand a squeeze. "I really do."

Wendy sure hoped her mother was right.

Nash pushed the triplets' stroller up the path at the far edge of the Dawson Brothers Cattle Ranch property. There was a beautiful view of the mountains here, and in all directions just trees and brush. This area was just a mile from the barn, but he felt as though he was in his own private world here.

It was why he'd chosen it for the site of his brother's memorial. Ethan, his wife and her parents were buried at the cemetery in town. Lydia had been the only child of only children, and they'd been the last of their family, so the Dawsons had decided to lay them all to rest in Bear Ridge instead of Cheyenne, where the Cannon family was from. Nash knew that his parents and grandmother visited the gravesites on the first of every month, but Nash preferred to come here, to the memorial.

A few days after the crash, Nash and his dad had driven back down to Cheyenne in his pickup and had hauled back everything that had been in their Cheyenne nursery, from the mini cribs to the books on the shelves, all of which he'd save for them since those things had been chosen for them by their parents. With his family's help, he'd gotten the nursery set up in the ranch house and with it done, with the sudden purposefulness of all that finished, he'd been beside himself and had gone out walking on the property, needing to feel grounded, to orient himself to this new normal.

A grieving, scared, shocked mess, Nash had walked to this spot, his favorite on the ranch, the place he'd gone often to think and work things out, and he'd found himself putting stones around an evergreen tree. Then he'd carved Ethan's full name, his birth date and the date that they'd lost him into the bark. He hadn't even been aware he'd been creating a memorial site until it was done, until he stood back and looked at the tree, at the carving, and had fallen to his knees and sobbed.

He came here once a week to talk to his brother. Ask his forgiveness, tell him how the triplets were doing, the milestones they'd hit that week, that month. Usually he came alone, but sometimes he'd bring the triplets. Nash wasn't the most spiritual of people, but he liked the idea that the triplets could sense their father with him, that Ethan could feel his babies present.

As he came around the brush that led to the memorial in the beautiful clearing facing the mountains, he was surprised to see someone else here.

His grandmother.

She stood before the tree, her walking sticks in each hand.

"Gram?"

She turned with a soft smile. "I can't believe it's

been six months. It feels both longer and shorter at the same time."

"I feel the same way," he said, pushing the stroller up beside her. He put his arm around her and they stood, their gazes on the tree.

He looked at his brother's name carved into the trunk. The dates. On this earth just thirty years. He closed his eyes, the ache in his chest unbearable.

"I was thinking about the last time I spoke to Ethan," Gram said. "Three days before the accident. I was telling him how excited I was that your mom and dad and I would babysit the triplets while they were all away for the rodeo event. I told him I loved him and he said, 'I love you too, Gram. Talk to you very soon.'" She sucked in a breath. "But that was the very last time."

Nash's heart clenched. "My last conversation with Ethan wasn't anything like that," he blurted out, the pain in his chest intensifying, his stomach twisting. He stared at his brother's name. The dates. And hung his head. "I told him that once again, he was being selfish, that he always put himself first. I was angry that he'd be away for Thanksgiving, that once again, he chose the rodeo over a holiday with his family."

His grandmother turned to him. "Nash. You never told me any of that. Have you been carrying around that awful memory for these six months?"

He nodded, unable to speak. "I was so resentful of him, how he just left us, left the ranch, to become a rodeo champ. I made him feel like hell about it. The last time we spoke—argued—was the day before the accident."

"Oh, Nash," his grandmother said, her voice full of compassion. "I'm sorry about that. But you can't beat yourself up about how you felt. You were entitled to your feelings on that subject. Just like I was entitled to feel differently about it. That's how the world operates. People see things differently."

He shook his head. "I was a jerk. And then he died. And I realized right away how wrong I'd always been. That I should have been his biggest champion. I know that now. It's why I have to let Wendy go."

His grandmother stared at him. "Let her go?"

He nodded. "I can't handle the thought of Wendy throwing away her dream, all her work and preparation for me. As much as I love her, she needs to fly, not have her wings clipped."

Livvy shook her head. "Nash Dawson, you listen to your gram. Wendy loves you and the triplets. She wants to be here. She wants a life with you and the boys. I know because she told me so."

"She told me too. But even if that felt right, I don't deserve it," he said in a broken voice. "I don't deserve her."

His grandmother looked so stricken at that, that those words had come out of him, that he wished he could take them back. But he'd known for six long months that you couldn't take anything back.

"So that's what this is really about, Nash. You're punishing yourself for how you treated Ethan by denying yourself the woman you just said you loved. But you're denying *her*. You see that, right? This is what she wants now. You and the triplets have become her dream."

His head was so jumbled. He could barely think straight. He hadn't seen Wendy or spoken to her in two days. He missed her terribly. So many times, he'd picked up his phone and tapped on her last text just to feel connected to her.

He put his hand on the stroller's push bar. Stared at the name Ethan Dawson in the tree bark. "Everything just feels…wrong, Gram. Every way I look at things, it just feels wrong."

"Promise me you'll think about what I've said. Things will right themselves, Nash. I believe that." She looked up at the sky, then back at him. "Think about what advice Ethan would give you right now."

He felt that in his gut. He remembered telling Braydon to think about what his mother would want for him. And the pushback he'd gotten from Braydon about that.

But thinking about what Ethan would want had been among Nash's first coherent thoughts after the news of the accident. And he knew the answer: for Nash to raise the triplets with everything he had in him. And he was doing that.

He felt his grandmother squeeze his hand. Then she moved over to the stroller and gave each triplet a kiss on the head. Callum let out a giggle. Ryder said, "La ba!" And Dallas started gnawing his thumb.

"If you want to know what I think," she said, turning to him. "It's that these babies are your present and future. You do have to let the past go, hard as that is.

Give them the *best* of their father, not your painful memories."

He instantly got defensive. "I'm very careful how I talk to them about their dad."

"I mean in general, Nash. You're tied up in knots over that last conversation. It's clearly haunted you for the past six months. Imagine how much more you can give these babies without all that pain inside you. Just imagine, Nash." She turned her walking sticks to the side. "Love you," she said, then walked on, back toward the ranch.

He stared after her until she disappeared around the curve in the path. Then he touched his lips and pressed his fingers to his brother's name and sat down on the ground beside the stroller. Staring out at the mountains.

And thinking. Despite how hard he tried to blot out his grandmother's words, they were echoing in his head.

Chapter Sixteen

At just before midnight, Wendy sat up against the headboard of her childhood bed, laptop on her lap, her notes at her side and a cup of chamomile tea on the end table. It was time to write the article. She'd put it off all day. Granted, she'd been busy with the farm, but she'd had pockets of time where she could have gotten started, including the past few hours. And she hadn't. In fact, she'd avoided going back to the house and her room—where her laptop was.

Because once she wrote the article, once she was finished with it and sent it off to Nash for his approval and got it back with his comments and changes, she'd be a few hours away from leaving.

Leaving Nash and the triplets behind.

Leaving her sister with a broken heart.

She shook her head in wonder at what was no longer on that list: *leaving without fixing her relationship with her mother.*

If anyone had told her days ago that she'd drive off from Bear Ridge with Andrea Watson in her corner, she never would have believed it. And now that they had this new closeness, she had a yearning deep inside to be around her mom. Who in a million years would have thought that her mother finally accepting her for who she was, being proud of her career, would make her want to stay? Wendy smiled at the utter irony of it all.

But leaving Tess when she was going through such heartache was rough for Wendy. She knew she'd just be a video call away, and at least they'd have the face-to-face. But being *really* face-to-face was better.

And then there was the man and three babies she loved with all her heart.

Once she had Nash's okay on the article, she would leave. No matter how she felt emotionally, she had responsibilities to the *Gazette*.

Wendy would have to go home. When suddenly it was Bear Ridge that felt like home.

Okay, come on, she told herself, grabbing her notes, which she really didn't need. She'd spent the past couple of hours going over the past several days in her head, remembering her questions, his answers, their talks, just being in his home, going through the steps, the routine of taking care of baby triplets.

She put her fingers over the keyboard. It was time to write.

For six months now, Wyoming has mourned the devastating loss of its home-state hero, bronc-riding champion Ethan Dawson, just thirty years old. The loss of Mr. Dawson, with his big dimpled smile, trademark tip of the charcoal Stetson and breathtaking talent on the back of bronc, was all the more heartbreaking because he left behind infant triplets, one month old. Those precious babies, Dallas, Callum and Ryder, were in the tender loving care of Ethan's retired parents and grandmother for the weekend. But when Ethan's twenty-eight-year-old brother, a single rancher running the generations-old Dawson Brothers Cattle Ranch, discovered he'd been named legal guardian of the triplets, he turned his entire life around to take in those babies...

In full disclosure, this reporter has known Nash Dawson since preschool and we were close childhood friends. When I heard that he had completely devoted himself to raising his baby nephews—from multiple nighttime wakings at different times, to making baby bottles and changing diapers, to learning lullabies, to rushing a feverish triplet to the pediatrician, to telling bedtime stories to waking in the glider chair in the nursery he'd created in his home more times than he count—I was not surprised in the slightest. That's Nash Dawson. A man of integrity, honor, commitment, dedication.

The day he got the heartbreaking news that his brother was gone, Nash made a promise not only to Ethan, but to his tiny children. To honor their parents and maternal grandparents' memories. To love them. To always put them first.

Nash Dawson had done just that. Dallas, Callum and Ryder are three of the happiest babies I've ever met. Sure, they've fussed and cried and flung their spoonful of oatmeal-banana at Nash's chin, which he licked off in good humor, but, oh, are those little boys well loved...

Wendy read over what she'd written so far. It was

just the opening and of the first draft, and she'd tinker, but it was a good start.

She took a sip of her tea, then wrote on about how Nash had learned to balance his new home life with running the cattle ranch, how his family and the community rallied behind him, always there to support him and lend a hand or drop off a casserole. Tears came to her eyes as she added a section of how he'd stopped dating to devote himself to raising baby triplets, to the steep learning curve involved. And how one day he'd only settle down with a very special woman who would love the triplets as he did. But for now, his heart was taken by three precious little boys who needed him.

Her heart snapped all over again at the thought that when and if he ever was ready, it wouldn't be her.

She drank more tea, kept writing, deleted a bit here, rewrote there, edited, reread, edited some more and then gave it a final once-over and polish, and then sat back and read it all again.

Done.

Her heart and soul were in this article. Her father, who'd instructed her to make sure of that from the time she'd written her first story in elementary school, would approve.

And even though Wendy had written the story as a reporter, with a mass audience in mind, she'd written it *to* Nash and the triplets, *for* them.

She sucked in a deep breath, then grabbed her phone and looked for her favorite photos of the ones she'd taken while at the ranch. One of Nash with the triplets, in their big stroller, in the barn, one of him standing in front of the mini-cribs, watching them sleep with the loveliest expression on his face. And three of the triplets solo, in their trademark colors, their different personalities so evident. There was Dallas looking intently at the squishy stuffed lion in his hand, Ryder with a huge smile that had *her* smiling right now. And Callum gnawing on his favorite teething toy, the little book with the rubberized edges.

She included three short videos, all under twenty seconds: one of them having their jarred baby food at the kitchen table; another of Nash lying down on the rug before the three cribs, telling them a made-up bedtime story; and one of him pushing the stroller up the path toward the barn, chatting away to them about the different kinds of trees on the property and the stately maple they'd just passed. Wendy had been trailing behind, having gotten permission to shoot some footage.

She watched all three videos with a hand pressed to her heart, tears flowing down her cheeks. How was she supposed to say goodbye? How?

Wendy closed her eyes and let herself have a moment, then took in a deep breath. It was time.

She opened the message window on her phone and clicked on Nash's name. She attached a copy of the article and the photos and the video, then typed: Attached is the article. As discussed, your eyes are the first to see this. Make any changes, however big or small, at your convenience. I've included three short videos and five photos.

All business. When every word of the article, the photos and videos, had become *extremely* personal.

Had she added the *convenience* thing to give herself more time here? He'd see that phrase and know he didn't have to read the story right away, that he wouldn't be holding her up. Maybe he wouldn't get to it for a few days since he'd been against the idea of the article before she'd come back into his life.

Back into his life. And out again.

What was that saying? *The more things change, the more they stay the same.*

In the morning, Nash still hadn't clicked on the attachment in Wendy's text—the article and photos and videos. He'd gotten the text at around midnight and had stared at it long and hard before setting his phone back on his bedside.

Make any changes, big or small, at your convenience...

He'd been grateful for the part about *your convenience*. He'd taken it to mean she knew he might not be up to reading it right away, the minute he got it. And that she wasn't waiting on his okay, that he could put it off till tomorrow. When he wouldn't have an entire long night facing him. His parents and grandmother were coming over soon to watch the triplets so he could get a couple hours of uninterrupted work in on the ranch. He'd read it on his way to the barn—when he wouldn't have too much time to think about what she'd written.

Last night, a few minutes after he'd gotten the text, he'd grabbed his phone off his bedside table and typed: Received. I'll read it in the morning.

He'd then stared long and hard at his own abrupt, sparse words, the words of a stranger, not a childhood best friend. Not someone who'd slept with Wendy Watson. And then pushed her out of his life.

Give her more, he'd told himself. *Something, anything.*

He'd then added, I wish things could be different, before he could think better of it or stop himself and hit Send, then tossed his phone on the chair in the corner of his room.

A ping had come a few seconds later. She'd texted: Me too. Maybe they can. Followed by a heart emoji, a smiley face in a cowboy hat and three baby faces.

He'd closed his eyes, holding the phone to his chest.

He must have drifted off at some point because he woke to the rooster, the sun barely up. He stared out the window, at the view of the pastures, then went into the nursery. All three Dawsons were still asleep. Dallas, Ryder and Callum, each so peaceful, their little chests rising and falling in their color-coded pj's.

He'd keep up that tradition, which his brother and Lydia had started. When they started walking, he'd get them tiny toddler sneakers in their colors. He'd stencil their names in their colors over their beds in their bedroom—he'd eventually switch rooms with them and give them the big primary so that they could comfortably share a room with three beds, three desks and three dressers, until they started asking—if they even ever did—for their own space. He smiled at the thought. He imagined the triplets so close throughout their childhood that they would want to keep sharing a room.

Unlike him and Ethan. Always arguing, fighting.

His parents had split them up when Ethan was eight and went to his first rodeo camp, forgetting anything else existed. Now Nash chuckled at how his brother had announced at dinner that he wouldn't be doing his chores anymore because he needed to go to the library to learn more about horses. Nash would wake up in the middle of the night and find his brother reading his horse books by flashlight. Their parents had always told Ethan, *Sorry, Charlie, chores first, then hobbies.* But when Ethan's talent became evident, they'd let him pull back from helping out on the ranch to devote his time to bronc riding. The way the Dawsons saw it, a special talent like Ethan had, whether sports or music or whatever, should be nurtured.

He now understood how lucky Ethan had been to have parents like theirs, even if he'd been stuck with a stick-in-the-mud, resentful younger brother who didn't get it. Nash would raise the triplets with his parents' outlook and let their interests and talents and dreams take them wherever they wanted. Even if that was away from the Dawson Brothers Cattle Ranch. Just as he'd told Braydon he would.

He took advantage of the fact that he was awake and up and the babies were still sleeping by taking a hot shower, getting dressed and then heading downstairs to brew some necessary coffee and make himself eggs and toast. By the time his parents and grandmother had come over, the triplets were in their high chairs, awaiting their jarred cereal.

As he said his goodbyes and gave each baby a kiss on the head, he'd felt his grandmother eyeing him and he knew she was wondering if he'd thought about what all they'd talked about. He'd been relieved to finally open up about his last conversation with Ethan to his gram, but he didn't want to think about what she'd said. About punishing himself. Denying himself.

Denying Wendy.

He didn't see it that way.

In fact, to prove that, he pulled out his phone. To read the article when he had no idea what it would call up in him, to look at the photos and videos, he'd be putting her first, focusing on her career. Not himself and how awful the past couple days had been without her in his life.

He went around the side of the barn that faced a fenced pasture, rested his arms atop the wooden slat, and clicked on the attachment.

For six months now, Wyoming has mourned the loss of its home-state hero...

The more he read, the more comfortable he felt. People would like the article. *He* liked the article. He'd always known Wendy was a good writer, but there was so much heart, so much depth and so many rich details about the intricacies of his day—from rising with the rooster or crying triplets, to getting the babies changed and fed and bathed and entertained, to his work on the ranch and how his loving family pitched in so that the triplets would be surrounded by family. He was amazed she hadn't been promoted several times over by now.

The day will come when Nash will feel ready to start dating, to open his heart and life to someone very spe-

cial, someone who'll love those precious triplets as much as he does...

Like you, Wendy, he thought. She was one in a million. He'd just gotten back his best friend—discovered that he could barely keep his eyes and hands off her—and he'd had to let go.

But it was good, he told himself. She'd go back to Cheyenne and achieve her career goals. The world was hers for the taking. That had always been the point.

He opened the photos, his heart both healing and cracking open. He watched each video three times.

Oh, Wendy. This will take you everywhere you want to go. He knew that for sure and it was all he needed.

He was about to text back that there wasn't a single word he'd change, that it was perfect, that he loved it, that it served as a beautiful tribute to Ethan, and that the triplets would one day read it and it would be like a big bear hug.

But she deserved more than a text. He would tell her in person. And then say goodbye for good.

At just before 7:00 a.m., Wendy was in the barn, adding fresh straw on the rubber flooring in the goats' stall when she heard a vehicle pulling up in the drive. For the past few days, every little noise had her looking outside, hoping it was Braydon who'd come to find Tess to tell her he'd realized that he had to deal with the root of his issue around having kids—and that to do the hard work necessary to heal, he'd need her by his side more than ever. But when Wendy looked out the long horizontal window, it was Nash who was getting out of his pickup.

Her stomach dropped. Was he here because he'd read the article and wanted to tell her—face-to-face—that it couldn't be printed? That it was too much—too personal? That he wanted so much changed she'd have to start all over again so she might as well *not*?

Okay, now she knew she was going too far since the man pushing her out of his life so she could achieve her career goals wouldn't drop a bomb on her article.

She sucked in a breath, lifted her chin and headed outside. She knew her article was good. Great, in fact. Her best work ever. If he had a problem with it, it was because her love for him and the triplets was in every word and that might be too much for him.

"Hi," she said as he came toward her.

He just looked at her for a moment, and she drank him in, his handsome face, the brown Stetson shading his eyes from the bright sun, how good he looked in that navy Henley shirt and jeans.

"Personally," he said, "I think your article should win a Pulitzer. Who do I call?"

Her heart almost exploded out of her chest. "You liked it?"

"Loved it. I knew you were the one to tell our story. It's so well written, Wendy. With so much heart and soul and depth. I love that some day the boys will read that article and it'll mean so much to them."

Oh, Nash. She was so moved she couldn't speak for a second. "That means so much to *me*," she finally said. *You mean so much to me. And so do Dallas, Ryder and Callum.*

"You'll be in New York or LA within a few months," he said. "I have no doubt."

"So you're just going to walk away from this?" she blurted out. "Walk away from what we have? I love you, Nash. And I love the triplets. There, I said it. I mean, I'm sure it was obvious from the article, but now you know. I love you and I want to be with you. You and the babies. I want us to share our lives."

He stared at her as though she were speaking a different language. And she realized why—because that was how badly he didn't want to hear what she was saying. He needed her to leave. For him to keep going, he needed her to be Ethan. He needed to champion her in Ethan's memory.

Her chest started aching, and her eyes filled with tears. This was beyond her. Because it was about him.

And if he was ever going to deal with how he felt, the pain deep inside, maybe she had to let him go.

"You know what I wish?" she whispered. "That you would see me as me. And not look at me, at us, through the lens of your relationship with your brother."

His expression changed. His frown was deep, brows furrowed. "So you have a long-time crush on a small-town rancher raising three triplet babies. A week—and one very passionate night—is going to make you give up everything you've worked your whole life for? To suddenly change diapers all day? Come on, Wendy."

Now *she* frowned. He really didn't understand. He just couldn't see past his guilt over his brother.

"I never said I'd give up anything," she said, her voice strained. "There are newspapers everywhere, Nash. Even in Bear Ridge. And any choice I'd make for myself would be valid—and to use your word, should be celebrated. People change, evolve, grow. That's *life*."

She looked away, angry, hurt, disappointed.

Crushed.

Speaking of...

"And another thing," she said. "Don't you dare call what I feel for you a crush. I'm not thirteen anymore. I'm in love with you, Nash Dawson. And I love those triplets with all my heart. Why is wanting to share my life with you and them any less important and meaningful than a promotion or a byline in a major newspaper?"

He slightly shook his head as if reinforcing his take on this. "I won't stand in the way of your lifelong dream to be a big-city journalist coming true, Wendy. Bear Ridge, marriage, kids, that was never your dream."

"And your life for the past six months wasn't either," she said. "Well, the ranch was. But not the triplets. Now you wouldn't trade your life for anything. Things change. Things *happen*."

He stared at her hard for a second, and she could see him trying to find his argument. She wouldn't win this fight. But neither would he. There was *nothing* to win. "But this—the ranch, this farm, me, the triplets—it's not your life and isn't meant to be. Your life is in New York or Los Angeles. Paris, even. Writing hard-hitting, news-breaking stories."

"You're not hearing me, Nash. What I want has *changed*. I want my life to include you and the triplets. Or is the real problem that you don't return my feelings?" she asked, her knees feeling wobbly. "You don't love me." Like always. Then and now.

She blinked away the tears threatening.

He turned away, looking out at the pastures, at the goats jumping on their logs.

"I guess I have my answer," she said, her chest aching. "You'd think I'd be used to it, but it kills all over again. Because I'm not just losing my best friend. I'm losing the man I want to marry. And the triplets my heart yearns to help you raise."

"Wendy, I—" But he stopped talking and just stood there, clearly struggling. "I never ever meant to hurt you," he said. "But this is goodbye."

She almost gasped. Not that she should have expected him to suddenly grab her into his arms and tell her he loved her too.

As he turned to walk away, her heart shattered and her legs did almost give out.

And when she heard the ignition turn in his truck, she ran inside the barn and climbed up to the hayloft like when she was thirteen—and sobbed.

Chapter Seventeen

Three days after that awful talk with Wendy, Nash couldn't shake his general mood: rotten. The only times he snapped out of it was when he was with the triplets so he tried to spend as much time with them as possible. He didn't want to think about how awful he felt, how much he missed Wendy, even their connection itself, which was gone, just like that. He had to stay busy, distract himself.

He'd needed to check the outer wood fencing in the pasture near the barn for warping and leaning and loose nails, so he figured the relatively mindless and physical work and being able to bring the triplets in their stroller would do wonders for his head. It was a beautiful day, low seventies and breezy, and the babies, lined up beside each other, were clearly enjoying themselves. Dallas was staring at Nash as he moved along the bottom board, looking for issues. Ryder was gnawing on his chew toy, which Nash was surprised he hadn't thrown yet. And Callum was giggling at the way the leaves on the big oak moved in the breeze. Every time he laughed, Nash found himself less tense, less upset. The triplets were the only antidote to his smashed heart.

At least his master plan had worked. Wendy's article had come out in yesterday's *Cheyenne Daily Gazette*, and social media had made it accessible all over. Folks had stopped him in town yesterday afternoon during a grocery run to tell him how touched they were by it. One elderly man, who Nash had always known to be quite taciturn, had put his arm around Nash's shoulder and squeezed, and there might have even been tears in the man's eyes. He'd headed home fast, his parent and grandmother nonstop talking about the article, how well-written and perfect it was, how proud they were of "their girl Wendy" and Nash.

He didn't feel proud. He just felt like hell. It helped that his plan would work; clearly people were reacting as expected to the story and someone in town had said it would likely go viral, that they'd soon see him and the triplets on the *Today Show*. Yeah—no. When the landline had started ringing yesterday, he'd shut the ringer off.

"Hey, Nash."

Nash turned toward the voice. Was that Braydon coming toward him? He lowered the brim of his Stetson a bit more against the glare of the sun. Yes, it was. Besides his family, Braydon was the only other person whose reaction to the article interested him.

Nash waved and wheeled the stroller over to meet him.

Braydon kneeled down in front of the triplets with a smile. "Hey, guys. I read all about you in Wendy's article online. Don't tell anyone, but I laughed at the part when you, Ryder, flung a glop of baby cereal at Uncle Nash." He laughed, then stood up. "That was really a great article. Put some things in perspective for me."

Nash stared at Braydon. "Oh, yeah?"

"The past several days I've been doing a lot of thinking. But I kept coming back to the same old conclusions. I was getting more and more torn up. Then I read that article and everything changed."

Nash felt himself brighten some. "That sounds like very good news."

Braydon nodded. "Since you and I had that talk, I kept thinking about how you said I should think about what my mother would want for me. It pissed me off for days and I tried to push it away, but the article made me see it differently. Like, yeah, my mom died, but my *dad* was great and I had him and my grandparents. And, yeah, Ethan died, but *you're* great and they have you and your parents and grandmother. And if God forbid, I die and my kids are without a father, they'll have Tess, the greatest woman on earth and her parents and sister." He smiled and shook his head. "It seems so simple, but I couldn't see it because I was so broken up about the losses themselves."

Nash put a hand on Braydon's shoulder. "I'm really glad to hear that. You and Tess are back together?"

"Not yet. I have a stop to make first. Jewelry store in Brewer for the nicest engagement ring I can afford. You're the first to know—don't tell Wendy!" He laughed. "I can't believe yesterday morning I was all twisted up in knots. Now, I'm about to propose marriage. And if Tess wants five kids, well, five it is." He kneeled down again in front of the stroller. "Thanks to you guys, I know that even three at once is manageable, so hey, what's two more? Hopefully not all at once though." He popped up. "I've got a ring to buy. See you later, man. And thanks. Really. You and Wendy changed my life, Nash."

As Braydon ran off in the direction of his pickup, Nash stared after him in amazement. He kneeled down himself in front of the stroller where Braydon had just been. "Wild, huh?" he asked the triplets. "I've gotta say, that feels good. Wendy and I got through to him in different ways."

He wished he could tell Wendy but he'd been asked not to—and he and Wendy weren't even friends anymore. She was out of his life. At his own doing.

He sucked in a breath and touched a finger to each baby's soft cheek. "You three look so much like your daddy. You've all got his eyes. Dallas, you have his nose. Ryder, you've got that something in the expression—Ethan Dawson one hundred percent. And Callum, you've got your daddy's smile. I love you three so much—"

Suddenly, he heard his grandmother's words echoing in his head. *Think about what Ethan would want for you...*

Nash realized he'd had it wrong all this time what Ethan would want for him.

Yeah, of course his brother would want Nash to raise the babies with everything he had to give. All his love. Devotion. Commitment. But Nash had always known that because Ethan had named him guardian—even if he had been second choice.

He now knew what he'd been missing. What Ethan really would want for Nash. His brother would want Nash to forgive himself. So that he could truly be there for the triplets.

It's that these precious babies are your present and future, he heard Livvy Dawson saying. *You do have to let the past go, hard as that is. Give them the best of their father, not your painful memories.*

He felt something creak open inside him. A window. A door. And a whole lot of feeling came rushing in. But instead of pain and regret, it felt warm and comforting.

And then some ideas suddenly streamed into his head. Ranging from a little out there to very possible. Hmm...

He looked at the triplets, his heart bursting with love for them. "I have some big thinking to do, guys. I'm gonna need you to be my sounding board, okay?"

"Ba la!" Ryder said.

Callum waved his hand around, the chew toy dropping to the ground.

Dallas giggled.

Nash laughed and grabbed the toy, putting it in his pocket, then wheeled the stroller toward the house, talking out his *new* grand plan.

Wendy sat at her desk in the bullpen of the *Cheyenne Daily Gazette*, putting the finishing touches on her new article. Her first big story since her promotion to full reporter, no *assistant* in her title anymore. After she'd filed the article from Bear Ridge and returned to Cheyenne two days ago, she'd met with Janna and the big boss, who'd informed her that the piece had exceeded their expectations and it would run on the front page in Sunday's paper. A *big* deal. They'd reminded her that it would be linked all over social media and she should expect it to go viral within hours.

They'd been right. She had five offers from news outlets ranging from small and big, including one in New York City, to send her résumé and clips and that they'd love to meet with her to discuss opportunities.

It was exactly what she used to dream of. What she used to want.

And now it was hers for the taking.

Except she no longer wanted it.

A part of her was thrilled that she'd done it. She'd gotten what she'd worked so hard for—a chance. But a bigger part needed something else now.

Home. Her family. And love. She'd have to work on that, actively go after it. But she'd have to wait on romance—for a long while. She knew she wanted a husband and children. But she'd first have to get over Nash Dawson and somehow stop thinking about the triplets every second of every day. She missed the four of them so much.

But she had to accept that Nash didn't love her.

She'd already given her two weeks' notice to Janna, who'd been very surprised but said that her feelings for Nash and the babies were in every word of that article and she got it. Janna spoke to the big boss, who said because she'd just been promoted a minute ago, she wouldn't have to give notice at all, she wouldn't be leaving them in the lurch, and if she could finish the current assignment, she could go any time.

Wendy was going home to Bear Ridge tonight.

One of the emails she'd gotten was from the editor in chief of the *Bear Ridge Free Weekly*—simply a very kind note about how much he loved her article and he'd always known she had a special touch with human interest pieces and he wished her all the success in the world.

She hoped he'd hire her when she stopped in tomorrow to ask for a job. But she had a good feeling about that.

She wanted to live in Bear Ridge, build her new relationship with her mother, help her sister plan her wedding—and boy, had Braydon come around—and work at the free weekly, telling stories like Nash's. Life-changing moments.

Yes. She was going home.

Her desk phone rang and she grabbed it. It was Nell, the *Gazette*'s receptionist. Wendy had a visitor.

She filed the article, her last for the *Gazette*, and turned off her desktop, taking a deep breath. The end of one chapter. Her studio apartment had come furnished, so she had very little to pack up and bring back to Bear Ridge. Tonight, once she got into her car, she'd start a new chapter. She'd rent an apartment in town, as close to the coffee shop and newspaper office as possible.

She'd probably see Nash and the triplets on Main Street every now and then. She had no idea what that would be like. They'd likely shake on being "friends," though she couldn't imagine being friends with Nash Dawson for a long time.

She glanced around the newsroom, then headed to the hallway and the reception desk.

And gasped.

Nash Dawson was sitting in the little reception area. He stood when he saw her.

"You're here?" she asked—stupidly. But she was so surprised it was all that came out of her mouth.

"I'm here," he said. "The triplets are back home with my parents and grandmother."

She stared at him for a moment, processing that she wasn't dreaming, that Nash was really standing in the little waiting area of the *Cheyenne Daily Gazette*. He looked so handsome, his expression markedly different than the last time she'd seen him. He seemed…hopeful.

And hope now bloomed inside her.

"I've worked out a plan," he said, taking her hand to lead her just outside the glass double doors into the hallway of the building. "The triplets were a great sounding board. I can tell I have their approval. And if I have your approval, I'll talk to my parents and grandmother about it—but I think they'll be fine with it. As long as—"

She tilted her head and held up a hand. "Um, Nash, fine with what?"

"If I hire a really great, experienced foreman to run the Dawson Brothers Cattle Ranch, I can work remotely as a ranch consultant since I have solid experience in turning around troubled ranches, including mine. I can work anywhere—from Cheyenne to start and then wherever your career takes you. New York, LA. This is if you'll even have me, after all I've put you through."

Wendy's mouth dropped open. "Wait. *What?* And hold on—you in New York City? Do they wear Stetsons there?" She smiled, her heart and mind very slowly catching up to his words, which she couldn't quite process.

Foreman for the ranch? Work remotely? From Cheyenne? From New York City?

"I do love you, Wendy Watson. I love you so much."

She gasped, her hand flying to her mouth, her heart now soaring.

"I was so blocked—by all my guilt, my heartache. All my regret. But a wise eighty-one-year-old's words and Braydon and some soul-searching and the excellent seven-month-old triplets all helped *un*block me. You were absolutely right, Wendy. People *do* change and evolve and grow. I didn't want to accept that because I needed you to be a stand-in for my guilt over my brother. I understand that now. And I'm done with it. I know what Ethan would want for me. And for his triplets. Forgiveness. From myself. And nothing but love and happiness and going after our hearts' desires. For me, that's you."

She burst into tears, then flung her arms around his neck. "You're mine too. But I guess you already know that." She kissed him with all the love and passion inside her.

"Oh, and I appreciate how much you're willing to sacrifice for my career, Nash. You'd give up running the ranch? Move here to the city? Move to New York?

With a triple stroller?" She chuckled at the notion of Nash pushing that behemoth down Broadway. "That's pretty amazing. *You're* amazing. But *I* already knew *that*." She smiled. "But turns out you won't need to do any of that."

His expression changed from happy to worried. His brow furrowed. "What do you mean? I thought—"

"I've already decided to move back to Bear Ridge. I gave my notice here this morning, as a matter of fact. And now that I've written my final story for the paper, I'm free to go. With my boss's very kind blessing. I want to be near my family—and I have so much to tell you there. I want to work at the *Bear Ridge Free Weekly*, and hopefully they'll hire me as a reporter. And I want you and the triplets. I want us to build a life together. The four of us. With our families."

Surprise and then relief washed over his handsome face. "Well, that's a big yes from me." He pulled her into a hug and kissed her again.

"You've found a way to balance home and work, and I'll do the same," she said.

He nodded. "We can make anything work—together."

She nestled her head against his chest, then looked up. "I love you so much. So, so much."

"I love you too, Wendy. And I really don't want to propose to you in the carpeted hallway of a building, but I want you to know that when we get home, I plan to get down on one knee by the creek at our favorite old spot near the river on the ranch and ask you to be my wife."

"I wonder what I'll say." She felt happy tears poking at her eyes and blinked, the man she loved so much standing before her with such love in his own eyes.

"The triplets are going to be really happy when they hear the big news," he said.

And then he kissed her again, every dream she'd ever had coming true.

Epilogue

On a Saturday afternoon in late June, the two brides were getting ready in the bridal tent set up behind a stand of trees at the Dawson Family Guest Ranch. Second cousins of Nash's owned the popular dude ranch and had offered them the beautiful back field for their double wedding. It was as if the weather gods knew there was a very special occasion for sunny skies and seventy-two degrees without a drop of humidity for good hair.

Wendy and her sister stood in front of the floor mirror, Tess also clearly trying not to cry as their mom made the final touches on their veils, then stepped back, her hand covering her mouth.

"You both look so beautiful," Andrea Watson said, her voice catching.

The brides both smiled at their mom in the mirror. They'd gone dress shopping together—the three of them. Their dresses couldn't be more different except for the color, white. Wendy's was strapless with delicate lace around the hem. Tess's was off-the-shoulder with beading around the waist. Tess wore her mother's veil, and Wendy wore Nash's mother's veil. They both had something old, something new, something borrowed and something blue.

A text pinged on their mom's phone. "Showtime, girls," she said, taking a final look at herself in the mirror. Andrea looked so lovely in her pale blue mother-of-the-brides dress. "Wedding march in thirty seconds. Dad's waiting for you just outside the tent." Her eyes misted. "I'll go take my seat before I burst into tears and ruin my makeup."

They gave their mom a last hug as single women. Then they took a final look in the mirror, made sure they were all set.

"I've never seen you look so happy," Tess said, grabbing Wendy's hand.

"Same for you," she said, giving a squeeze. "It means so much to me that we're doing this together. Sharing this day."

"You're gonna make me cry," Tess said, fanning her face.

Wendy smiled and did the same. "Okay, let's go find Dad."

They hurried out. Their father stood just outside the tent flap, looking so handsome in his pale gray suit. He also teared up at the sight of them.

"You both look so beautiful," he said, swiping under his eyes.

"Aww, thanks, Dad," Wendy said.

With him between them, they each wrapped an arm around his, and as the wedding march began, they moved around the stand of trees and down the beautiful white runner that led to the ceremony site.

They'd tried to keep the wedding small, just family and close friends, but the guest list had kept growing and they'd given up. Since it was a double ceremony, Wendy's guests were on the left and Tess's on the right. She saw old friends and newer ones, including her former boss, Janna, and her new boss at the *Bear Ridge Free Weekly*, Henry, and her new coworkers. In the front row on Nash's side were his parents and grandmother in a beautiful peach-colored dress, many Dawson relatives, and friends from town and the ranching community.

And standing up at the small stage were their handsome grooms in their tuxedos, the minister behind them at a podium. Braydon looked so happy, his gaze on his bride, tears shimmering in his eyes.

She tried not to cry with happiness as she shifted her attention to Nash, who watched her come down the aisle. She was marrying her dream since she was twelve years old. Her childhood best friend. Her rock and her champion.

Just to the side of Nash was the triple stroller with three adorable babies in tuxedo pj's that Nash's parents had found in a gift shop.

As they neared the stage, Wendy looked at her groom, all his love reflected in his blue eyes. In minutes, she would say *I do* to the man she loved and to the three babies who'd had her heart from the first minute she met them.

And to the happy, full, busy life she couldn't wait to begin—together.

* * * * *

Get up to 4 Free Books!

We'll send you 2 free books from each series you try PLUS a free Mystery Gift.

FREE Value Over **$25**

Both the **Harlequin® Special Edition** and **Harlequin® Heartwarming™** series feature compelling novels filled with stories of love and strength where the bonds of friendship, family and community unite.

YES! Please send me 2 FREE novels from the Harlequin Special Edition or Harlequin Heartwarming series and my FREE Gift (gift is worth about $10 retail). After receiving them, if I don't wish to receive any more books, I can return the shipping statement marked "cancel." If I don't cancel, I will receive 6 brand-new Harlequin Special Edition books every month and be billed just $6.39 each in the U.S or $7.19 each in Canada, or 4 brand-new Harlequin Heartwarming Larger-Print books every month and be billed just $7.19 each in the U.S. or $7.99 each in Canada, a savings of 20% off the cover price. It's quite a bargain! Shipping and handling is just 50¢ per book in the U.S. and $1.25 per book in Canada.* I understand that accepting the 2 free books and gift places me under no obligation to buy anything. I can always return a shipment and cancel at any time by calling the number below. The free books and gift are mine to keep no matter what I decide.

Choose one:
- ☐ **Harlequin Special Edition** (235/335 BPA G36Y)
- ☐ **Harlequin Heartwarming Larger-Print** (161/361 BPA G36Y)
- ☐ **Or Try Both!** (235/335 & 161/361 BPA G36Z)

Name (please print)

Address _____ Apt. #

City _____ State/Province _____ Zip/Postal Code

Email: Please check this box ☐ if you would like to receive newsletters and promotional emails from Harlequin Enterprises ULC and its affiliates. You can unsubscribe anytime.

Mail to the Harlequin Reader Service:
IN U.S.A.: P.O. Box 1341, Buffalo, NY 14240-8531
IN CANADA: P.O. Box 603, Fort Erie, Ontario L2A 5X3

Want to explore our other series or interested in ebooks? Visit www.ReaderService.com or call 1-800-873-8635.

---

*Terms and prices subject to change without notice. Prices do not include sales taxes, which will be charged (if applicable) based on your state or country of residence. Canadian residents will be charged applicable taxes. Offer not valid in Quebec. This offer is limited to one order per household. Books received may not be as shown. Not valid for current subscribers to the Harlequin Special Edition or Harlequin Heartwarming series. All orders subject to approval. Credit or debit balances in a customer's account(s) may be offset by any other outstanding balance owed by or to the customer. Please allow 4 to 6 weeks for delivery. Offer available while quantities last.

Your Privacy—Your information is being collected by Harlequin Enterprises ULC, operating as Harlequin Reader Service. For a complete summary of the information we collect, how we use this information and to whom it is disclosed, please visit our privacy notice located at https://corporate.harlequin.com/privacy-notice. Notice to California Residents – Under California law, you have specific rights to control and access your data. For more information on these rights and how to exercise them, visit https://corporate.harlequin.com/california-privacy. For additional information for residents of other U.S. states that provide their residents with certain rights with respect to personal data, visit https://corporate.harlequin.com/other-state-residents-privacy-rights/.